"HAPPY NEW YEAR, MICHAEL," LAURA SAID, TRYING TO CONTROL HER FEAR.

Michael looked at her with rage. "If you just dropped in to celebrate New Year's Eve, you can forget it. You might as well get out of my bed and on the next flight back to California."

She tried to turn her face from his fury but found she couldn't. He held her too tightly against the covers. "I need you," Laura whispered, trying to make him understand. "I've come to stay."

He stood up then. "And I've needed you. I've been insane with needing you. Loneliness for you has been eating my guts out."

CANDLELIGHT ECSTASY ROMANCES®

MORE PRECIOUS THAN GOLD

Cindy Victor

A CANDLELIGHT ECSTASY ROMANCE®

Published by
Dell Publishing Co., Inc.
1 Dag Hammarskjold Plaza
New York, New York 10017

Dell ® TM 681510, Dell Publishing Co., Inc.

Candlelight Ecstasy Romance®, 1,203,540, is a registered
trademark of Dell Publishing Co., Inc., New York, New York.

ISBN: 0-440-15827-3

Printed in the United States of America

First printing—April 1985

For my own hero: Gary

To Our Readers:

We have been delighted with your enthusiastic response to Candlelight Ecstasy Romances®, and we thank you for the interest you have shown in this exciting series.

In the upcoming months we will continue to present the distinctive, sensuous love stories you have come to expect only from Ecstasy. We look forward to bringing you many more books from your favorite authors and also the very finest work from new authors of contemporary romantic fiction.

As always, we are striving to present the unique, absorbing love stories that you enjoy most—books that are more than ordinary romance. Your suggestions and comments are always welcome. Please write to us at the address below.

Sincerely,

The Editors
Candlelight Romances
1 Dag Hammarskjold Plaza
New York, New York 10017

CHAPTER ONE

Laura Daniels came home so dog-tired that she couldn't even muster the energy to scratch her cat's head.

"If I bend down, I'll fall down," she explained softly to Mouser, who was normally extended the courtesy of a good scratch when Laura entered the house. Laura wearily climbed the sweeping staircase to her bedroom, with the cat following her.

It's going to hurt to go in here, Laura thought as she approached the bedroom. It did every night, but tonight would be much worse than usual.

Washing up for bed, she peered into a mirror that for six months of nights had reflected a lonely woman. Strange, she thought, that the loneliness hadn't altered her appearance. This afternoon a friend, with whom she lunched at the expensive Le St. Germain, had said Laura looked more beautiful than ever.

Loneliness must become me, Laura had thought at receiving the obviously sincere compliment, but instead of voicing that bitter sentiment, she had smiled and said thank you. There was nothing to be gained by making people feel uncomfortable or by wallowing in self-pity.

She could honestly say that she hadn't given in and wallowed once today, and for that she felt she deserved congratulations. *Well, on your wedding anniversary you should be congratulated on something,* she thought. When she awakened this dreaded morning, she had quickly given herself a silent but forceful lecture on not giving in to unhappiness. And she hadn't faltered. That didn't mean she hadn't prayed every time the phone rang that it would be Michael. But every time she answered and it wasn't Michael she responded to the caller with a cheery sound in her voice.

And a stone in her heart. With that stone firmly embedded she went to Zale Winters's cocktail party. Several of the famous author's male friends made her aware that she didn't have to endure unending loneliness, the unrelenting pain caused by Michael's absence.

Zale Winters had tried fervently—again—to let her know that she didn't have to be lonely.

But she did. Michael—no one else—could take away her loneliness. So instead of going on to dinner with Zale, she had returned alone to her Robertson Boulevard studio. *Who said living alone leaves you with idle hours?* she'd wondered, looking at her desk. She knew, though, that the mountain of work was just what she needed. Grateful to have it, she had sat down to a Friday night of one task followed by another. There was a story on an ultraluxurious Newport Beach development to be finished for *Decorating Age,* a living-room design to be worked up for a client who wanted no involvement with decorating her own Bel Air mansion, fabrics to be pored over with knowing, critical, yet appreciative eyes. Laura loved the materials she worked with and the results she achieved.

Working on the magazine article gave her a grim sense of irony, for all that she truly enjoyed writing about interior design. It was through her journalistic endeavors as a decorator that she had met Michael. She'd gone to his "architecturally pure" Mediterranean estate home in Beverly Hills to do a piece on it for *Decorating Age.* Now she

10

lived in it. But she lived in it alone except for Luisa, the maid, whose spacious room and bath were downstairs, off the service porch.

The work at hand gobbled up Friday night, as she'd wanted it to, and she didn't lock the studio and climb wearily into her moss green Mercedes until well after eleven. Michael would never have permitted that. He had been even more hungry for her time than her career was, and their evenings had always been spent in each other's company. And in a whole lot of other people's company, too, she had to admit.

Michael would also never have allowed her to leave the studio alone and get into her car unescorted late at night. He had protected her as if she were the earth's most precious gem.

But he'd left, and she lived in a huge house protected only by a security system.

Laura finished washing up, reflecting on the long day and evening. Mouser sat stoically on the white wicker clothes hamper lid, regarding her.

She turned off the bathroom light and went into her bedroom. The draperies hadn't been pulled closed, and moonlight gave a soft luster to the room's exquisite furnishings. There was enough light to undress by, and Laura, nude, turned down the bedcovers. To turn down the bed was one more ache in her daily routine. Michael used to do it. He liked to be in bed first and watch her come to him. He'd said that for her to come to their bed either nude or clothed in a luscious gown that clung to her curves—a gown that he had chosen for her—made her look wanton.

Michael had loved to buy lingerie for her. On their wedding night, five years ago, he had confessed to being indecisive on whether he himself wanted to take Laura's peignoir off or watch as she did it for him.

Tonight, without turning on a bedside lamp, Laura pulled open a dresser drawer and indifferently extracted a lilac gown.

Then, shattering her indifference with a stifled sob, she put it back and withdrew the one beneath it. She hadn't worn the white satin gown that Michael gave her on their last anniversary since he left her.

She held her breath as she remembered the look of love in Michael's eyes when she came to him wearing this gown on that joyous anniversary. By holding her breath momentarily, she kept from sobbing aloud. Oh, how he had looked at her and caressed her when she wore this for him. Beneath the spaghetti straps the gown clung to her body down to her hips. From there it overlapped provocatively till the long slit curved away from her ankles in a softly rounded hemline. Lace covered her full breasts and extended in a diagonal panel across her belly and over one hip.

On that last anniversary Laura had not known whom the gown's lace was intended to tease. Her rosy nipples had strained against the lace as if wanting to burst through that which separated them from Michael's hands.

Laura had dreamed of walking into their rose garden, dressed in the nightgown, to be made love to by Michael while gazing up at the stars. It would have been to experience heaven. When she moved into the house as a bride, that had become her fantasy. She had never walked in the yard without thinking that she should tell Michael her fantasy of making love under the stars. It would have delighted him, and he would have made it become reality. But she never had.

Laura raised the gown over her head and let it fall into place around her love-starved body as if it were a shroud. Michael had killed her perfect happiness by leaving her.

She stood still, not wanting to get into her lonely bed. Like a bad joke, the opening strains of the time-honored "Anniversary Song" played in her mind.

Oh, how we danced on the night we were wed.

They had danced, all right. And after dancing, and laughing, and loving each other with their eyes and hands, they had made love until the stars drenching the universe with light seemed to be under the ceiling of this very room.

We vowed our true love, though a word wasn't said.

Words *had* been said, and she could remember every one of them. She crossed her arms over her chest and clutched herself in anguish as Michael's words of love whipped across her memory like steel blades.

Stop it! Stop thinking about him! He isn't thinking about you, she told herself. Oh, but he must be! Never mind that he hadn't called today. He *must* be!

Laura ran her slender fingers over the diagonal lace panel of the gown almost involuntarily. She wondered if he ever pictured her wearing his anniversary gift. Tonight, as this anniversary came to its bleak close, he could be thinking of the last one—of her in this gown.

She caressed it again, feeling the softness of the material. Michael loved soft things: negligees and roses and the curves of her body. He loved to touch her lips with his fingertips and put his face against her shimmering honeyed apricot hair.

But he loved hard things, too: ores from the earth's dark interior. He had given her this gown. But soon after, he had given her a type of mineral, a hematite, to celebrate the day they met. She could not know, as she unwrapped the curious but stunning gift, that it portended the end of her world.

Laura let her fingers drop down against the thigh that Michael would never stroke or kiss again. He wouldn't be

13

back. She still wore her wedding ring, but it mocked her. Its value could be measured only in dollars now, and memories. Today she had stared at it and wondered if it wasn't time to take it off. Time even to divorce. Why not? She had thought about it rationally. It would be best to do it before another anniversary hit her like a ton of bricks. Maybe after divorce anniversaries were less painful. Maybe.

She would not think about it tonight. Tomorrow's schedule would be brutal if she didn't get some sleep. She got into her side of the bed. She still slept only on one side, falling asleep almost in prayer that by some miracle she would wake up and find Michael next to her or that she would awaken in the night to the sound of his key in the lock. She didn't expect ever to hear that sound. Who really expects miracles? But she needed to believe that he hadn't thrown the key away. Somewhere—in some corner of a dresser drawer—it would lie useless, eventually forgotten.

She was afraid that this would become one of those nights when she couldn't sleep at all, when her eyes would be turned toward Michael's smooth, unused pillow in the dark. Michael had said he loved her eyes because they were intelligent, humorous, loving, and turquoise. Especially because they were turquoise. He had joked that her turquoise eyes had lured him into eternal love.

Eternal love. A lie.

She closed her eyes and vowed not to open them again this night. She must sleep. Saturday was a working day, and at the end of it she would feel exhausted. Besides, Saturday night there were two parties that she *must* attend. And on Sunday . . .

Sleep, she commanded herself. Enjoy soft, sweet sleep. No memories. No longing thoughts. No wild fantasies of waking up to find Michael beside her or of hearing his key in the lock.

She willed herself to relax deeply. *Just sleep; it's so easy to do if you let yourself.*

Sleep.

A noise suddenly jarred her alert.

She sat up in the bed as the sound of the front door-knob's being turned broke the stillness a second time. Even Mouser, who had been asleep at the foot of the bed, was erect and alert.

Was a key turning in the lock? Oh, God, was it Michael?

No. No, that was a crazy thought. Someone else had gotten a key somehow. This was not a dream coming true; it was a potential nightmare.

Laura quickly lowered her feet to the plush peach carpet, her body tensed and torn by conflicting impulses. Instinct told her to stay still, make no sound, to stay hidden and possibly safe. But at the same time something in her wanted to rush to her home's defense, to confront fear and conquer it.

She snatched up the gift from Michael—the hematite that she kept on her nightstand. It was the only thing she could think of to use as a weapon. She knew she couldn't actually hit anyone with it; she wouldn't have the guts to come that close, and even if she had, she wouldn't have enough physical power to do much damage. But by God, she could throw the thing.

And probably miss. She left her bedroom praying that this was a false alarm.

At the top of the curved stairway she stopped and stood in heart-pounding silence. The stairs and the entry hall to the left beneath it were not blessed by moonlight as her bedroom was. The blackness that swallowed up even Mouser's form was ominous enough, but when a footstep in the shadows broke the eerie quiet, Laura gasped in response.

"Who's there?" she demanded, and was surprised that she could actually speak.

There was no answer. Was it Luisa? Laura wondered. Luisa had a key to the house and knew how to deactivate the security alarm before using it. But Luisa would answer. And Luisa hadn't gone out tonight. Had she? Laura had assumed that the maid was in and already asleep when she herself had come home late and tired. No, she was sure it wasn't Luisa.

But it could be Luisa's new boyfriend, a heavy drinker of whom Laura strongly disapproved. Luisa might have given him her key to the house, or more likely, he could have ferreted it from her handbag. And now he would be lurking in the shadows of the foyer, drunk and undecided whether to run or stay.

Laura began walking down the stairs, one hand holding the mahogany handrail, the other clenched fearfully at her breast. "Who is it!" she snapped, more than asked, followed by "Julio? Are you there?"

She fervently hoped so. If it were Julio, and he were drunk, she might be able to gain control of the situation. But if it were someone else, he would be wise to say, *"Sí, señora,"* and then take off into the night.

Mouser meowed and then purred. Yes, Laura had heard correctly. The cat did it again. He purred and purred. Laura almost lost her footing on the stairs. Only one person in the world could evoke that sound of contentment from the aloof cat, she thought, her heart pounding.

Before Laura could cry out in a combination of relief and fury, he lunged from below. Her trembling body was clasped against the hard form of a man who had no intention of fleeing into the night.

His mouth came down over hers. In spite of her anger at having been put through harrowing fear on top of every-

16

thing else, Laura met the hungry masculine lips with an urgency of her own. The arms that held her infused all of her body with sensual wakefulness, as if a magic potion were being poured into the mold of her being. In her loneliness she had been hollow as a woman, and the rough, firm grip on her body promised that the void would be filled to bursting, the aching need quieted.

Yet she struggled. An inner voice, the one representing all her suffering, cried, *Damn you! Damn you!* even as she desired him. That voice waged war against the desire, trying to overpower and kill it.

He crushed her against his chest as if sensing the war going on inside her. He held her so tightly it seemed the lace over her curves and the rough wool cloth over his hard musculature would be fused into one fabric.

Laura writhed against him to free herself. He held her only more tightly and roughly parted her legs with his strong thigh. If the gown hadn't already been slit, the force of his thigh would have rent the cloth. As it was, Laura felt the denim that sheathed his leg rub hard against her bare skin.

His mouth released hers and slid across her cheek to the lobe of her ear, and he breathed his need hoarsely. Then he nibbled at the small diamond that dotted the perfect pink lobe.

Beloved Michael had himself put that diamond, and its twin at her other ear, there. He had slid the silver post that thrust from its mounting through her lobe, secured it, and then lovingly traced the gentle curve of her ear with his knuckle. That had been three years ago.

Now warm, moist urgency mocked the gentleness of that remembered caress. But dear God, she had needed Michael's touch over the cruel half year that he had been

17

gone, and her yielding breasts—stilled now against the chest softly crushing them—were admitting that need.

But the hands feeling her blood-roiled flesh were not the smooth, finely manicured rich man's hands that had been there before. They were rough, calloused, and more demanding than anything Laura had ever known against her skin. She thought he might be aware of this and delighting at the contrast between the rough hands on her now and those that had last touched her. If he gave it a thought, it was a cruel thought, but everything happening to her was cruel. She wanted to scream at him for all the cruelties—and beat against him with her fists. But she could not fight. She was vulnerable and in need, and he had entered the night to claim her.

Laura went limp in his arms at last and felt herself being lifted. Her arms went around his neck in submissive obedience. Wordlessly, staring into each other's eyes, she and her seducer ascended the stairs to the elegant master bedroom. No man this raw and blatantly masculine had crossed that threshold since Laura had lived in the house. Only beautiful, beloved Michael had. Michael had never been soft, but his masculinity had always had the stamp of elegance on it. Looking into the clear gray eyes of her seducer, in the moon's soft light, Laura realized that this was a mountain man, a loner at home with forest streams and raw weather. He didn't belong to this pampered puffed-up pebble of the globe, where Rolls-Royces, Ferraris, and Mercedes nested snugly in clean garages.

But looking, as if entranced, into those wide almond-shaped eyes, Laura sought and found a tender answer. The lovemaking of this unexpected visitor, despite his roughened hands, would be all reward and no punishment. A half year of loneliness would be healed and forgotten when he possessed her.

And so she would give in without protest. He put her on the bed and leaned over her. His balled fists were firmly positioned at each side of her splayed lush hair on the satin-encased pillow.

Laura didn't say a word, or expect him to. What could be said between them? He didn't have to ask her for forgiveness. Then, very slowly, with cool, arrogant enunciation, he said, "You are mine." As he said it, he opened one fist, only to close it again in a crushing grip on the gown's lace bodice.

The words, or the threat to what Michael had given her with his love on their last wedding anniversary, snapped Laura out of her entranced submissiveness. Drawing her knees sharply up in self-protection, she snarled, "Like hell I am!"

Both her small hands caught at the hard, massive one gripping the lace vee between her breasts. When he loosened his hold in surprise, she wrenched to the side and in two swift movements had turned over, like a cornered animal protecting its tender belly from attack.

In turning over, she had forced his knee off the bed, and he now stood tall beside her. She could feel his gray eyes burning into her skin from that height. The relentless stare would have seared her flesh if it hadn't been for the protective gown. Laura now knew that a bare whisper of cloth could be a mighty shield, and this beautiful white one was serving her well. When she turned over, it had caught tightly behind her knees, so that it was stretched tautly over the quivering curve of her back and hips.

For moments he had not moved or spoken, and his breathing was so silent he might have vanished from the room, as Michael had one morning. When Michael left, she had lain on this bed, staring up at the ceiling, making no more sound in her grief than a rose makes in dying.

19

Now she was silent, too. If he didn't move, she wouldn't. If he didn't speak, she would not cry out. If he didn't breathe, she wouldn't either.

Then without warning his powerful, calloused hands gripped the nightgown's straps, one at a time, and ripped them from her shoulders. Laura felt his knuckles positioned against her back, and then the nightgown—the beautiful gift from Michael—was torn like some old sheet. He ripped it from the top to the base of her spine, and Laura heard a low groan escape from him as she was exposed.

Laura sobbed. But the sob was soothed away from her throat by a sensation unlike anything she had ever felt. Softer than an angel's kiss, something caressed her nape and trailed slowly down the center of her satin-smooth back until it had traveled the length of her. She shivered in anticipated ecstasy, knowing that whatever had touched her would be followed by the sweet torture of gentle but purposeful kisses. *Yes,* she begged in silence, hungry for the thrills to come.

It didn't happen. Laura heard the movements of clothes being slowly removed.

He knew, then, that she would struggle no more, that he could take as much time as he pleased with her, that whenever he was sated, it would be too soon for her.

He put his hands on her head and stroked her silken hair.

Let the night never end, Laura prayed.

His fingers caressed her neck, first moving the shoulder-length swirl of hair off it, as once Anne Boleyn's dark tresses had been moved to expose her soft white skin to the executioner's gaze. This tormentor towering above Laura's naked form, though, was here to awaken life, not to still it. When he repeated what was undoubtedly true—"You are

20

mine"—she reached her hand up behind her neck to clasp his fingers. She drew his hand beneath her face and turned it upward so she could kiss the palm. If there was any other gesture of submission necessary, she didn't know what it was.

"Turn over," he said, and she instantly obeyed.

Her turquoise eyes, which had flashed earlier with rebellious rage, were so clouded by desire now she could hardly see clearly. He was a blur of breathtakingly handsome features. The room, which on her wedding night had let the stars come in for Laura, was in gauze. It was as if clouds had sensed there was more drama in this single room than in the whole night sky and, curious, had come inside to see the show.

"Do you want me?" he asked, lowering thickly lashed eyes to gaze at first one and then the other naked breast.

Laura's whispered "yes" was so soft it was without sound. Her fingers tremblingly explored the dark hair around his flat nipples. He took one and then the other slender wrist in his firm hand and raised her arms above her head.

"Keep your arms just as they are until I say to move."

He began to kiss her, starting at one alabaster wrist that was still in his grasp. He kissed it until she felt as if her wrist were melting into the satin pillow. Then he moved his lips down her arm to the shoulder.

Laura thought the sensual kisses on her shoulder would be followed by his head grazing down her throat and chest, but that was not the case. He languidly began again at the other wrist, so that when at last he came to the second smooth shoulder, she felt nearly faint from longing. She obeyed him as to the position of her arms, not lowering them to grab fiercely at the thick brown hair that her fingers yearned to be buried in. But she couldn't lie still. She writhed at his teasing tongue and lips on her engorged breasts, and she arched her back when at last his mouth came hungrily down over her soft belly. His hands gripped her hipbones as he kissed her—gently first, then thrusting his tongue at her navel. He moved lower, spreading her thighs so he could look at her. Then he traced infinitely soft circles with one knowing finger beneath her pelvic mound.

He stopped abruptly. Laura had to bite her lip to keep from crying out and begging for more.

"Beautiful lady," he murmured, in a tone as deep as Laura's hunger, "did you want this all the time? From the moment I grabbed you on the stairs?"

"Yes! Oh, yes!" She willingly admitted it, whipping her head from side to side. She had promised not to move her arms, and he was once again holding her pelvis firmly against the bed. *Something* had to move. Even her toes were arching, in greedy anticipation of the kisses he would bestow upon them when he was done taunting her.

And at last Laura's toes did receive their fair share of kisses. Even the soles of her small feet were blessed with his caress. When the tip of his tongue lazily made a tour all around one foot, Laura's other ankle sought the strong masculine neck and rubbed against it as an enraptured cat would seductively move against a scratching post.

He laughed—rich, joyous laughter—at that brazen caress and nipped at the heel of the foot he was holding with perfect white teeth.

Then he took her.

He kept the promise made when Laura yielded against him on the stairs and allowed him to lift her up in his strong arms. The void of loneliness was filled; the painful months were chased from her memory.

When all passion was spent, when he had gone limp

22

inside her and was staying in her soft, rich, sheltering warmth for sweet rest, it was Laura who finally broke the silence of bliss.

"Welcome home, Michael," she murmured against her beloved's shoulder.

She had won. Her prayers had been answered. He was home. The pain was over. Happiness spread before her like a victor's heralded march into conquered land.

"Happy anniversary, darling," she whispered.

Michael raised himself from her slowly. Kneeling astride her, he reached an arm out to turn on the bedside lamp. He lifted what he had caressed her bare back with an hour ago.

"Careful of the thorns," he said warningly.

Laura laughed lightly and took the young rose he held. So the angel's kiss along her spine had been the lip of a shyly unfolding rose petal. She placed the pink curling bud against her white breast, so that the fragile petals caressed her nipple.

"You're so beautiful," Michael said after scrutinizing what was displayed for him alone to admire. "So beautiful."

CHAPTER TWO

Laura had a thousand questions, but when Michael responded to the first one with "Let's not talk about anything tonight," she agreed. It was best not to break the mood.

It was also time to sleep. The night that she had prayed would never end *would,* and at its end she would have to get out of bed and go to work. That she felt happy for the first time in months would not matter one little bit to a client trying to decide how to decorate his living room.

She tried not to think about anything but soon found she couldn't stop.

A hundred things flashed through her mind. But the one thing she didn't want to think about was that the coming day held a full schedule for her, plus two dates in the evening.

She had to attend one party out of love of friends who had been exceptionally dear to her since Michael's leaving. The Harrises didn't treat her like an abandoned soul or an object of curiosity, as many well-meaning acquaintances did. They just tried in many little ways to give her moral support and help her keep her chin up. They were having a cocktail buffet Saturday night to celebrate the completion of their remodeled kitchen and refurnished dining room. Laura wouldn't have to stay long, but she would have to go.

The second party was being given by a long-standing client who wanted to introduce Laura to a European woman who had just purchased a Bel Air mansion and a Palm Springs condominium. She couldn't pass up an opportunity like that.

Oh! Zale. She'd forgotten. When she had refused to go out for dinner with him after his Friday night party, he had made her promise to have lunch with him. He had said he would come by her studio at one and wouldn't mind being kept waiting if she were tied up.

That one she could get out of. And possibly one appointment could be rescheduled for Monday, leaving her a few hours to spend with Michael early in the day. And in the evening . . .

No, she would sleep now and worry later. It was something that merited worry, though, because the partygoing and endless evening obligations had been part of the reason that Michael had left. He had broken the news to her on a Saturday night—following a huge party, a theater date, and an after-dinner supper with five other couples.

She remembered. Oh, how she remembered! She had been lying in bed that night, and she had murmured sleepily that it had been a hectic weekend.

Michael had responded dryly that their whole life was hectic.

No more, she warned herself. If she started remembering, she would start hurting and resenting. This was not a night for that. This was a night for love and peace. And tomorrow night should be, too. She would be totally insensitive to Michael's needs if she asked him to go to two parties the first night he was home with her. The sacrifice he had made for her, in coming home, was huge. The least she could do was cancel those two blasted obligations. But . . .

"You're not sleeping," Michael said accusingly, gently massaging the breast his hand had been resting against.

"I'm too excited," Laura said. Really, how dare he expect her to sleep through the predawn hours after all the excitement, joy, and passion that had come like a gift of midnight?

"Maybe we should talk now," she suggested. She would probably have to meet the day without having slept at all anyhow. And Michael could sleep in the morning after she got up.

"Nope. I don't want to talk now. We have all day and tomorrow night for that."

Laura winced, deciding quickly that she would forgo the second party. Michael would certainly understand about the Harrises. He had always liked them. They would stay for just an hour.

"Tell you what. Since *I* don't want to talk and you can't sleep, why don't we . . ."

He finished the suggestion with his thumb's drawing a lazy circle around her nipple. Laura smiled, sighing simultaneously, and arched a foot against Michael's leg. Oh, how good the crisp, curly hair on his shin, and the deliciously smooth skin it covered, felt against her toes. While appreciating that sensual treat, she felt his arousal against her. But then it seemed to falter just a little.

"You've got to respond with more than your cute little foot, woman, if you want to keep a guy who's traveled all day and been up twenty-two hours going. It's an hour later in Hisega, remember?"

She remembered, but the word "Hisega" was anathema to her. She hated the very sound. As a place-name it had slightly less charm than "Siberia," slightly more than "hell."

Michael had explained that six little girls once named

26

the beautiful countryside where they were picnicking Hisega, an amalgam made up from their first initials. The name had stuck. Now Hisega was a very small village nestled by a meandering creek. Rugged people who loved the wild outdoors, needed privacy and space, owned horses, and fished for their suppers lived there.

Laura knew little else about it except that it was close by many unspoiled lakes, where no development was permitted. And in Hisega Michael had lived for six months in a cabin that was part of a ranch.

No, she had no love for the word "Hisega." The only other word she hated as much was "Keystone." Michael had described that village as the gateway to Mount Rushmore: a few streets of touristy shops and restaurants that bustled with activity during the frenzied tourist season and were quiet the rest of the year. And in that mountain gap, flanked by an old-fashioned candy shop and an Indian arts and crafts store, stood The Ornery Ore, Michael's rock and mineral shop. Wishing no living person any harm, Laura would have waved a magic wand and removed Hisega and Keystone—and all of South Dakota for good measure—from the globe if she could have. It had taken Michael from her.

Michael had said that western South Dakota was *real*. Real people lived there, struggling with winter while wearing boots and parkas and relishing their freedom.

But Laura knew that real people also lived in Beverly Hills, California. Real people shopped at Neiman-Marcus and Saks as well as at The Ornery Ore. Real people were grateful for a smog-free sky over Los Angeles now and then and thanked their lucky stars if they could get parking spaces on Rodeo Drive. But they didn't worry too much about the smog and congestion. If they wore boots,

27

it was to be fashionable, not because boots were a sensible means of keeping feet warm and dry.

But she wouldn't think about all this now. He was here, home with her. The nightmare was over.

So, apparently, was his offer of seconds on lovemaking. The soft, rhythmic breathing that moved his hard chest gently against her back told her that he was asleep. *Sleep for both of us, darling,* she thought lovingly. She would get out of some of her commitments this weekend. Maybe the Sunday brunch could be canceled—unless Michael wanted to go, of course. Maybe he would welcome a sumptuous brunch at the Beverly Hills Hotel after eating whatever it was that people in Hisega ate. Buffalo maybe, she mused. Venison stew and deer jerky. Pheasant. Lots of trout. She smiled, wondering idly if Michael had come back to Beverly Hills hungry for her or good food. Well, she didn't care why he had come back; she just felt as if her home had become Eden, a garden in which there would never again be pain.

Had he sold The Ornery Ore yet? Or would he have to go back there to make arrangements? She wouldn't like that. She didn't want him in South Dakota again. He had loved the place; everything about it revitalized him, he had said.

As if he had needed revitalizing. Michael was the most dynamic man Laura had ever met. Just being around him revitalized others and gave them a standard of purposefulness, charm, sincerity, and discipline to measure themselves against.

No, she didn't want him going back there at all. He might—horrible to imagine—decide he had made a mistake in returning to Beverly Hills.

And I couldn't live through the torment again, Laura thought.

Somehow, as that thought trailed away, Laura slept.

She had set her digital clock radio to go off at 6:15. But when she awakened, it was not to the soft music of KJOI. It was to the sound of her bedside phone. Laura grabbed for it, certain in the first fuzzy second of wakefulness that she had slept half the day.

"Laura? Zale. I called your office three times and was beginning to wonder if you had forgotten to get up this morning. I knew you left my party tired, but were you *that* tired?"

"Zale! What time—?" She looked at the clock. Dear Lord! She would never be able to apologize adequately to the people she had stood up, especially since one had driven in from Rancho Mirage to see her.

She quickly got rid of Zale, who, on hearing that Michael was back, mustered the grace to say, "That's great, just great, Laura! Give him my best, and I hope to see the two of you soon."

She hung up wondering if she should call and make a stab at apologies or first make the call canceling one of tonight's parties. Hearing Michael get out of the shower, she decided she should forget everything else and run downstairs to tell Luisa to fix him breakfast. He must be starved by now.

"Hi, Rip Van Winkle. I thought you wouldn't get up until it was time for me to grill our dinner. I was looking forward to serving you dinner in bed."

"Michael! How long have you been up?" In spite of feeling harried, Laura breathed in contentment at seeing his beautiful body fill the dressing-room entrance. He hadn't bothered to wrap a towel around his waist after drying off. Michael would never do that. Laura had teased him once that someday he would give Luisa the shock of her lifetime. He had responded in playful vanity that Luisa would

29

sing lustily while she dusted and mopped on that momentous day.

"I've been up and about for two hours, my love. I ran and lifted weights, and then Luisa fixed me a breakfast fit for a king. The neighborhood sure looks great. All the gardeners deserve a round of applause. It's funny, seeing flowers in bloom in December and everything so green. Back home it's barren."

She nodded, smiling. But why had he said "back home"? Just a phrase, a turn of words that held no meaning, of course.

"I haven't lifted weights in so long I had to remind myself to take it easy. Thanks for keeping the weight room intact for me. I know you don't use it."

"Why wouldn't I have kept it? I always knew that someday . . ."

Her voice trailed off because she was lying. She hadn't known that someday he would come back to her. And she hated to be dishonest, especially with Michael. Actually she had expected him to send for the weights. If he hadn't soon, she would have donated them to a boys' club because seeing them depressed her.

"Gosh, you look good, darling," she said to change the subject. "You must have worked out a lot . . . back there to keep in shape as you have."

He patted his flat belly, where a thin line of dark hair extended down from his muscular chest. "No, I don't work out now. But I haul and chop my own wood. I've taken up climbing—with somebody who's really gung ho about that, somebody very special. And I ski. I still run in the morning, more because it's so damn gorgeous outside than for keeping fit. I ride Misty as often as I have time to, but that exercises her, not me. It's funny, Laura, that here

30

I had to lift weights to keep in shape, but now I can keep in shape naturally."

Laura nodded, trying to appear interested, but she licked her upper lip in apprehension. Michael was telling her something—something she dreaded knowing. He was telling her, using the present tense, "I haul and chop my own wood. I ski." He hadn't said, "I hauled," and "I chopped," and "I skied."

He was talking about tomorrow and next month and next year, not the past. He was . . .

Dammit! She swallowed convulsively and suddenly felt very cold and alone again, more alone than she had ever felt.

Michael came to her and took her hand in his, obviously understanding what she was going through.

"Laura, Laura, angel. I gave you no reason to think that—"

"No!" She jumped up off the side of the bed and pushed him away from her.

He allowed himself to be pushed, knowing that she needed a moment to be away from him, a moment to absorb the shock. But then he put his hands on her shoulders to steady her, and the powerful gaze of his gray eyes, beneath brows still damp from the shower, seemed meant to hold her up—to keep her from collapsing at the blow he had dealt her.

She whipped her head to the side, suddenly infuriated by that gaze. *He* wasn't going to hold her together! She would cave in if she wanted to! *He* wasn't going to decide how much she could endure. And he wasn't going to touch her anymore.

She dug at his hands to force them from her shoulders. How dare he touch her now? What gave him the right? Love didn't give him the right. The love was all on her

31

side, not on his. He *didn't* love her. If he insisted he did, then he was pitifully blind to what real love was. She had known that six months ago, when he left her to go live in the Black Hills of South Dakota with *real* people, subjecting her to *real* pain.

And what he had done last night had been cruel. He hadn't raped her body, but he had raped her soul. How could he cause her so much pain?

"Oh, Laura. Laura, baby, I love you so much. Don't push me away. Don't ever do that, honey, because I love—"

If he hadn't cupped her face in his hands, Laura might not have slapped him. But the combination of loving words and a loving touch was too much. She aimed well and hit hard. Her hand stung as if Michael's hard jaw had attacked it—not the other way around. She quickly sought anger in his eyes but didn't find it. She saw compassion, maybe even pity. And whereas his newly shaved jaw was tinged with heightened color only where she'd struck it, her face was suffused with the blush of grief. His eyes weren't even smarting, but hers glistened with tears. His jaw was firm; hers quivered. He was always the strong one, the man she looked up to and revered. But now she would be strong. First, she would have the strength to apologize. Then she would excuse herself and go take a shower. Then she would go to work. She didn't haul and chop wood, run, climb, ski, or ride a horse, but she had her way of keeping fit, too.

"Laura, no matter what you think, I love you."

He said it simply and with conviction. She ignored it and taking a deep breath, said, "I'm sorry I hit you, Michael. Really, I am."

She tried to walk past him to the bathroom, but he shot an arm around her shoulders and easily brought her in

32

against his chest. He held her there, feeling her breathe and sob and hurt.

"That's it. Cry first. Then we'll talk. The shower can wait."

"No, let me go, please," Laura said, sobbing. Reluctantly he released her, and she walked away from him. He had just professed his love for her, she thought, yet they were as alienated from each other as it was possible to be.

She did not come out of the bathroom after she had brushed her teeth. She got into the shower, having to stifle a sob when she looked for a moment at the wet towel Michael had used to dry off. How often she had looked at his empty towel bar. Now the bar wasn't empty, yet she was racked with grief and rage.

In the shower Laura poured shampoo into her still-smarting cupped palm, then lathered her hair with it. Her hands were trembling.

The stall door opened. "Let me," Michael said, beginning to massage her scalp gently. Not another word was spoken. He helped her rinse her hair, lifting thick, sudsy hunks up under the water as she leaned her head back. Then he gently washed her throat, shoulders and breasts, abdomen—everything down to her feet. When he stood back up, he kissed her lightly on each eyelid, then said, "Turn around." She did. As he massaged rich lathery soap onto her shoulders and worked down, she couldn't keep herself from saying, "This doesn't change anything. It doesn't stop me from hating you."

"Does this?" he asked softly as he gently massaged her buttocks.

"No."

"This?"

She gasped and felt a thrill course from the back of her throat to the backs of her knees as he eased the lather between her thighs. But like a child who isn't going to give in no matter what, she snarled, "No!"

"Play hard to get then. See if I care. You're clean anyway." He gave her a gruff hug with both strong arms and then turned the water off.

When he grabbed a towel to wrap her drenched hair, she stood docilely and let him do it. Then he took a second towel off the rack and began to dry her.

"You're wet, too," Laura said tartly.

"I know that. I just feel like spoiling you."

"You just feel like spoiling my life!" She snatched the towel from his hand and, after shooting him an angry look, turned her back. She rubbed vigorously and assumed he was drying off behind her. When she turned around, he was still standing still, looking at her in amusement—still dripping wet. But he looked so good, so boyish for all his lofty wisdom and thirty-eight years that she wanted to grab him to her and never let him go. Instead, she said sullenly, "Are you going to stand there dripping wet all day?"

"There aren't any more dry towels, Laura."

"I'll get one." She wrapped the one she had just finished using around herself and secured it above her breasts.

When she came back from the dressing room with an oversize navy blue towel, Michael said, "I washed you. How about drying me?"

She hadn't heard a better suggestion since last night, when he told her to turn over on the bed. But she couldn't abandon her mood of sullenness, couldn't behave as a friend or a lover to him because he wouldn't behave as a husband. "I didn't ask you to wash me," she said flippantly, flinging the towel at his chest.

Laura began to walk out of the bathroom but on the second firm step found herself naked. Michael had whipped the damp wrapping from her body. And before she could even move, he'd flipped the towel smartly against her backside.

"Are you having fun?" she snarled, whirling to face him and curling her lips around the words derisively.

"Not particularly. I'd rather spend the morning, or what's left of it, with a grown woman. But you'll have to do. I'm playing your game, little girl."

"Well, the game is over, Michael!" she almost shouted. "So now you may dry yourself off, pick up your marbles, and go home. You do have a home to go back to, don't you? Some cabin, or cave, out where men are men and women are drudges? I, in the meanwhile, will dry my hair, apply my makeup, and then get dressed. I have to work today."

"And party tonight?"

She faltered for only a second, then snapped, "Yes! And I'm having lunch with Zale Winters."

Maybe it wasn't a lie. She could call Zale back. Something could be salvaged of this miserable day. She hadn't forgotten Michael saying that he climbed with somebody very special.

"Mmmm, Zale Winters, eh? Yes, your decorating jobs do so often lead to personal relationships. Well, Zale's a hell of a writer. Do you see him often?"

"I see him when I see him."

Michael's eyes were locked onto hers, and she looked down for a second. Her sharp retort was unlike her, she thought. Michael had been right: She was playing a childish game. And she was painfully aware that she was being an excruciating brat. She firmly decided to act like a mature person and tell Michael that she and Zale were only friends. But Michael squelched her good intention by drawling, "And has he seen you as I'm seeing you right

now? You've been showing all this spitfire while quite naked, *Mrs.* Daniels."

She was sorry she'd already slapped him. It wasn't likely
that she would do violence to him twice in one lifetime.
"Draw your own conclusions, *Mr.* Daniels," she said sullenly, and she turned her naked back on him.

Luisa turned to beam at Laura, who had come briskly
into the kitchen, and said, *"Es bueno, señora, eh?"*

She was referring to having the lord and master back.
Luisa should only know that Mountain Man had merely
stopped by to tear a nightgown in two, Laura thought. But
Luisa would adore Michael no matter what he did. Ever
since he donated an exquisite brand-new suit and shoes for
Luisa's brother to wear at his wedding, the housekeeper
had adored him. Actually all the men in Luisa's family
wore Michael's cast-off clothes. He had been a true
clotheshorse before trading silk, worsted wool, and camel's
hair in for plaid flannel shirts and snug-fitting jeans. He
hadn't owned Michael Daniels—the ultimate in fine men's
clothing—of Beverly Hills, Corona del Mar, and Santa
Barbara for nothing.

"I fix eggs. Bacon. The jelly toast." Luisa boasted of
what she had done for her hero. Laura declined Luisa's
offer of duplicating this feast, said good-bye, and left the
house.

She got into her Mercedes as bleakly as if it were her
tomb. He would be gone, she was sure, when she came
back. Now she had the whole day and night to herself, not
to mention the rest of her life. She could go to six parties if
she wanted to. She could do whatever she wanted to do.
"Why?" she cried out loud, gripping the steering wheel so
hard her fingers whitened. "Why is he doing this to me?"

She opened the car door and got out, then stormed back into the house.

She ran up the stairs. He wasn't in their bedroom or the room that he had used as an office. She rushed back downstairs and headed for the weight room. Empty. So was the den that opened onto the brick patio in back. "Michael!" she shouted in frustration.

"I'm in here, having coffee," he called back mildly from the kitchen.

Laura eyed him coldly. He sipped at the strong black coffee, looking good-naturedly at her. Luisa, noting the look in Laura's eyes, quickly hung up her dish towel and hustled from the room.

"Luisa tells me she has a new boyfriend," Michael said in a mild-mannered tone, infuriating Laura further.

"He's a drunk."

"Oh? Too bad." Michael broke off the conversation to bend down and scratch Mouser behind the ear. Mouser purred gratitude and love. The cat, which Michael had bought because its fur was a close match to Laura's hair, had always adored its master.

"Mouser doesn't realize that you've abandoned him in favor of a horse," Laura said archly, offended beyond reason by Michael's nonchalance.

Not taking the bait, Michael asked, "How's your mother? I should go see her today."

"She's fine. She's in Hawaii. When she gets back, I'll tell her you said hello. Michael. *Michael!* Why did you come back here?"

"To give you the rose for one thing. I found it in the Denver airport. I had to go to Denver, and when I saw that rose—on the day of our anniversary no less—I re-routed and came here." He shook his head in wonderment. "It was beautiful. Don't you think?"

37

"I can't believe your gall. The rose is wilted, Michael. It's dead."

He shrugged and shook his head lightly.

She wasn't going to fly off the handle, not again. Calmly she asked, "Was there another reason to come back? One that makes sense?"

Her last words competed with the sound of Michael's chair banging to the floor. He had got out of it in rather a hurry. He crossed the room to her before she could catch her breath, and taking her shoulders in his hands firmly, as if to prevent her from fleeing, he answered.

"To get you," he enunciated slowly, through clenched white teeth. "To get you, you idiot. You're coming back with me."

CHAPTER THREE

Something in Laura, something fundamental, cried out to her to listen to Michael, to heed him, and, most of all, to be cautious because his fierce desire and love for her might not withstand further rejection.

Something that tumbled back through generations of women loving their men begged her to tell Michael that she would follow him, follow him anywhere on earth.

What, really, would be more difficult? Life without fabulous interior design options, and without nouvelle French cuisine, and without endless summer, and without two or three hundred close friends who also led exciting lives—or life without Michael?

Give in. Do it. Go with him, she told herself even as the hollow word sprang from her throat. "No!"

Their eyes met, and Laura wondered if she could retract the ugly word. It was so hideous. Who would think one word could do so much damage? But the word had taken on life of its own. Laura could no more recapture and harness it than she could catch and cage a moonbeam.

Make me do it, she pleaded silently, staring fervently into his gray eyes.

She even thought for an instant that she would be happy in South Dakota. Michael would see to that. If he were to treat her only half as lovingly—or a third, even a quarter

—as he had during their years together as man and wife here, her happiness would be assured.

Michael took his hands from her shoulders and stepped back. It seemed to Laura that this moment of loneliness and separateness would decide her future. She wondered if his hands had actually touched her for the last time. He could walk from the room and the house now and never look back.

But it was not the final physical contact between them. Michael raised one hand to Laura's hair, to stroke it gently from the top of her head down to where it ended just above her shoulder. He touched it as if he might not feel it ever again. Then he put his hand against her throat, and he moved his thumb down the side of that silken smooth column as if in wonder that the hateful word had actually come from this beautiful, elegantly scented part of his beloved.

Their eyes were locked in an embrace that seemed to meld his gray to her turquoise.

"Why, Laura?" Michael asked, not taking his hand from her throat.

She could feel her pulse racing against his fingers. It was as if her very blood were trying to convey to him that the word she'd uttered was the wrong one.

"You know why," she managed to say thickly. "It's all old territory. There isn't anything we haven't gone over and over and over."

She was surprised that she'd been able to get all that out. Her mouth was so dry. Her voice was so tired.

"Yes, but tell me again. Tell me just once more, Laura, and make me understand." His thumb caressed her throat again, as if prodding the reluctant words from her.

She swallowed and licked her lower lip. "It was all arbitrary, Michael. You didn't ask me, or even *talk* to me, before making your decision. My feelings just didn't count. My life didn't. But your decision—made without consulting me—turned my world over. It did whether I went with you or not. I was in a no-win situation, and if I went with you, the move would negate what I was, cancel everything I knew how to do, erase all my friendships."

It was more than she'd expected to say. But she'd said it well and was relieved that she'd been able to do it. She could credit herself with not whining, with not having spoken hostilely. She had just expressed the truth.

Michael took his hand from her throat and laid it softly against her cheek.

"You silly fool. You remarkably intelligent dear fool. How did you get so muddled in your thinking so young? You're only thirty-one. Dear Lord, Laura, nothing—*nothing*—not I, not South Dakota could cancel all the lovely things you know how to do or erase any of your real friendships. Nothing can negate you—your passion for life and love. But things can diminish you, darling. A frivolous, glittery veneer over your life can corrode it, just as if your life were a precious gem. It's more than that to me. Your life is more precious than gems."

He had stopped talking and took his hand from her face. He touched her hair again, and she restrained a sigh of gratitude. "This is so beautiful," he murmured, and he leaned forward to kiss the hair laid over his palm.

That brought the first tear over the brim. Michael had always loved her hair. She willed the tears not to flow and her voice to be steady. "Well." She began in a reasonably clear tone. "That—that isn't exactly old territory. You've never expressed any of that to me before. But it doesn't change anything. I won't—I *can't*—go with you, Michael. So, are you going to leave today?"

It occurred to her as she asked that question that he

needn't. All right, so her happiness wouldn't be permanent. In this crazy world whose happiness ever was? But a little happiness was better than none. Michael could stay with her awhile. A few days. A week. However long he wanted to.

"Yes. I'm going to leave today, Laura. I have to get home. There's no sense in prolonging this. If you need me, you know where I am."

She wouldn't respond. Anything she said would probably sound hateful. *If* she needed him, she thought. If he only knew.

"I'd stay, honey, if I thought by staying I could change your mind. But I don't think I can. When I said I was taking you with me, I envisioned some sort of Wild West scenario of hauling you onto the plane like a trussed calf if necessary. But that one little word from you had a solid sound to it. Your 'no' was pure metal. My staying another night won't change it. Anyhow, I promised someone I'd get back as soon as I could."

That someone special, Laura thought. It didn't add up. Why would he have come here for her if "somebody very special" were waiting for him in South Dakota?

But she wouldn't ask. If he wanted to elaborate, he would. "Well, good-bye then," she said. "I'm going to the studio, so have another cup of coffee if you like, before leaving. And go through the house and take anything you want, Michael. Oh, I just thought: Do you want Mouser?"

Laura had just noticed that the cat was sitting demurely in the tunnel that Michael's knocked-over chair created over the kitchen floor. The cat had always favored Michael, so he might as well have it.

Michael grinned. "Are you offering me cat custody?"

"I guess." She grinned, too. If they could part with smiles, it would come close to parting with dignity.

42

The grin quickly left his face, though, and he regarded her with stern features.

Why, Laura wondered, *do I feel about three feet tall when he looks at me like that?* She sensed that something that would not make her feel comfortable was coming. She wasn't perceptive enough, though, to imagine just how uncomfortable it would make her.

"Why don't we have a child to discuss custody of, Laura?"

"Wha—I don't know what you mean!"

His gaze grew sterner. His eyes had narrowed, and his sensually chiseled mouth had become a taut wire. A muscle tensed far back in his jaw. His features and even the muscles hidden by his beautiful smooth skin seemed to condemn her.

But she had a credible defense. "We were married only five years!"

He shrugged. "Certainly long enough to make a baby. We weren't children when we got married. We were responsible and solvent—affluent, if you will—adults. We were in love and capable of creating new life out of that love. So why, Laura, are we only talking about custody of *this?*"

His arm shot out to point at the cat so unexpectedly that both Laura and Mouser opened their eyes wide with surprise. The cat ran. Laura had to stand there and take it.

But she didn't have to talk.

He answered for her, in brief questions underscored with contempt. "You weren't sure? You weren't ready? You had a career?"

"That's right! But I would have been ready soon." Her jaw quivered now, and her eyes were swimming in tears. "It's true, Michael. I wanted a baby, too, and thought about it often. We wouldn't have waited much longer."

43

"A moot point now," he said without softening his features.

Laura had had enough. She squared her shoulders and snapped, *"Our* sex life wasn't Spartan, child or no child! And you weren't exactly a loner. You had your share of obligations, too. I'll bet that a good half of the invitations came from people coveting the company of *the* Michael Daniels, clothier nonpareil!"

"All true. But everyone who bought a foulard tie or hankie at Michael Daniels's didn't purchase my personal friendship with it."

"I don't make friends with everyone I meet!"

He nearly smiled. At least it seemed to Laura that his jaw had relaxed a bit, and his eyes grew less severe. "No, not everyone, my love. They make friends with you. And those that don't become intimate chums have to make do with dinner party acquaintanceship. Oh, Laura, you can't help it if people surround you because you're so terrific. But you *don't* have to let them get so close that you suffocate."

"I think you're exaggerating," she said primly, knowing full well that he wasn't.

"Mmm. I considered going into the Christmas card business and selling my whole stock to you. I'd have died a rich man."

"You already were a rich man," she said, reminding him. "This is getting us nowhere. I don't think it's fair of you to bring up why we didn't have a baby. And I'm not killing myself with work and stress. Nor were you. I love what I do. And you sure loved being in business for yourself. You still *are* in business for yourself. You changed your product and your address, but that's all you changed, Michael."

He raised a brow, silently asking her if she really

44

thought that was true. She didn't. Well, she had lost the war, so she might as well get banged up in a few more battles. She started the next one with "Just because you were a frustrated geologist shouldn't mean I have to give up everything my life consists of! Dammit, Michael! You could have had a mineral collection right here! I'd have let it take over the whole living room!"

He threw back his head and laughed. Before, when his strong features softened almost into a smile, she had been relieved. But his laugh worried her.

"Don't you laugh when I'm letting off steam! What I'm saying makes sense! Look, Michael, I love beautiful furniture. Most furniture made in America comes out of North Carolina. So what if I'd just popped out one day with 'Michael, I'm closing my studio, and you'll have to sell your business because we're moving to North Carolina so I can . . . so I can . . .' "

She faltered, not sure where her reasoning was leading her. Then she blurted, "So I can be a carpenter and make beautiful furniture!"

His laugh was hearty, and his eyes gleamed with mirth. Laura was going to sputter another protest against his having fun at her expense when she realized just how silly and tangled her logic had gotten. "Well"—she sighed, with the beginnings of a sheepish grin playing on her mouth—"go ahead and laugh. My premise was sound anyhow."

"Laura," he said when he was able to stop laughing, "if you'd come up with an idea like that, on some Sunday night when we'd just finished a weekend of six social engagements, I'd have whooped for joy. Honey, give it up. Come with me, where you belong. Do you think there is anywhere on earth where we wouldn't be happy together?"

She didn't. As long as she could be in Michael's arms,

the Black Hills of South Dakota would be as exhilarating as Paris, as sensual as Tahiti.

"Change your mind, Laura. Say yes. You want to. You're right on the edge now. I can feel that you are. Come on, baby. Do it."

She had always been cooperative, the kind of person people called good. She had obeyed her parents and teachers. Rebellion had not been part of her makeup. But something in her that was as powerful as her ability to love— maybe more powerful than it—was not going to let her be ruled by another human being.

"No. I'm not going," she murmured, and then after several long seconds of hesitation she continued. "And I think we should divorce."

Dear God, had that come out of her mouth? she wondered, shocked at her own words.

Michael snorted in derision. "You do that. You divorce me, Laura. Go to an attorney; go to that divorce lawyer, Mark what's-his-face, that we met at the Coopers' party, and tell him you want to file for divorce. Then tell him about last night while you're at it. Tell him how when we make love, the planet changes course."

"I'll tell him how you changed all the rules," Laura said sullenly. "Good-bye again, Michael."

She turned and walked out, feeling an odd need to concentrate on the mechanics of walking. *Just put one foot in front of the other—that's it—and walk away from your life,* she instructed herself.

But life would go on. She would meet the challenge. She would do what she had always done—even if it meant getting into bed alone. For the rest of her life.

That's how it's done, Laura, when life goes on, she told herself. She turned the key in the ignition.

CHAPTER FOUR

It was after ten on New Year's Eve when Laura's plane set down at the Rapid City Regional Airport. Laura had an aisle seat, but she'd been able to get a look out the window when the plane began its descent.

Rapid City was isolated. Except for the occasional lights of farms there was only the blackness of uninhabited land; then came the cluster of lights of a small city that stood alone.

Laura had lived all her life in Beverly Hills, California. That was a city within a city, and radiating outward from it in every direction were other cities. Those in turn touched and blended into other cities. This complete isolation of a community was phenomenal to her.

The older man sitting next to Laura, who was a grandfatherly sort, said, "Did you know there was some talk awhile back of renaming this the Gutzon Borglum Memorial Airport?"

Laura had not known; she doubted if many people did. She also doubted if the name of this airport was something she could muster up any interest in right now. There was only one thing on her mind and room for nothing else. Michael. She would be with him soon. Only a few weeks had lapsed since their second parting, but those weeks had seemed every bit as long as the half year separation that preceded them.

Laura had nearly come apart during those bitter weeks. Finally, *finally,* she had realized that no remedy except being with Michael would hold her together.

So she was here, waiting to get off a plane in South Dakota. But other people, with their own histories of joy and sorrow, were also waiting to get off. Laura could see that several minutes would go by before she was free to walk from the plane to the terminal. She listened politely, feigning interest, as the man explained that some of the people in Rapid City had felt renaming the airport after the sculptor of Mount Rushmore would be a proper way to honor him. But the majority opinion had been one of opposition, and so a Gutzon Borglum memorial still had to wait its turn.

"That's interesting," Laura said, but she anxiously eyed the solid line of people standing between her and South Dakota. She felt that while she was still on the plane, she was not yet on the ground of her new state, her new home. Home. From this moment onward South Dakota would be her home. She didn't know what life held in store for her here, but she knew that life would be good. With Michael life was always good; without him it was hell.

"Just a few moments, and you'll be out in the snow, young lady. Don't you have gloves to put on?"

Laura smiled and said that she didn't but that it didn't matter. *Snow,* she thought. Imagine that. Being Southern California born and bred, she had never seen snow fall before. She had been to places where there was snow, but it had always been on the ground by the time she got there. The way it really looked during its descent had always been a mystery.

Then, after the sluggish line of travelers had finally left the plane, Laura found herself climbing down metal steps in a snowfall. The air was very cold, and she quickly learned that not having gloves *did* matter. Well, she would learn these lessons as they came along. She walked fast, but not just because she was freezing. Every hurried moment would bring her to Michael that much quicker. She hoped fervently, as she entered the terminal where no one was waiting to meet her, that before the hour was past, she would be in Michael's arms, that the distance to Hisega wouldn't be far, that there would be some sort of transport service, and that she would get out of the airport quickly.

There was a service, called Airport Limo, she discovered. The driver, who stood beside Laura as she waited for luggage to appear on the carrousel, told her that the distance was very far, that in this weather it would be a long, slow drive, and that sometimes "you wait half the night for them to get the baggage off the plane."

He was more talkative than the man next to her on the plane had been. "It'll be an hour and a half, probably, before we get to Hisega. I'm dropping that couple over there by the phones off at the Hotel Alex Johnson. That's in town. If we weren't stopping in town, we'd take Omaha and over to Jackson. But we aren't going anywhere till the baggage starts moving." He nodded toward the barren carrousel and shrugged. "Takes forever sometimes. Looks like tonight's one of those times."

Laura told herself that she couldn't do anything about it and might as well stay calm. She could not run back to the plane, climb onto it, and claw her suitcases off. Nor could she shorten the distance to Hisega. So she would just try to relax.

After a few minutes, however, she wanted to scream. Instead, she stared hard at the carrousel and tapped her foot.

"Someone waiting for you in Hisega, to ring the New Year in?" the driver asked.

Laura thought the question was presumptuous. She also thought the answer would depend on what was meant by "waiting." She nodded, though, and tried to make her lips into something resembling a smile. It was one of those bunched-jaw, tight-lipped smiles that people gave while coping with the ironies of their fate.

Oh, please, she thought, *let me be there before midnight. Let the New Year be started as it should be, with Michael's arms around me and mine around him. And with a kiss.*

She had to wait awhile longer, but all at once the moving carrousel was laden with quivering luggage of every size, color, and stage of deterioration. Laura's suitcases stood out among the others, and several people looked admiringly at the pale blue leather that had not so much as a scratch on it yet.

Michael had bought this luggage when he and Laura were planning a holiday. But then he had left her, and the suitcases, along with Laura's happiness, had been shelved. They were being used for the very first time now. Laura's mother was shipping the rest of Laura's belongings to Hisega.

When they finally got into the van, Laura was happy to discover that the driver had willing conversationalists in the couple he was taking to the hotel, so she was left to her own musings for the first twenty minutes of the journey. She looked out her window at falling snow. How lovely a gift it was to have this new experience on the eve of her brand-new life. Surely the enchanting snowfall was an omen that while life here might be strange to her, it would also be beautiful. She put her hand on the window that she peered through. She felt as if every snowflake were falling to make her happy and that every light that shone in the quiet town were lit to welcome her.

What was Michael doing this very second? She wondered if he, too, was watching the snow and appreciating its beauty.

If he was occupying himself as she was, the comparison between them stopped right there. For while she was ecstatic to be on her way to him, he didn't know she was coming. Perhaps he expected the moment of one year ending and another beginning to be bitter with loneliness.

Laura felt sorry for him. *Oh, hurry!* she thought. Did the driver really have to move this thing so slowly? It was snowing, but did that mean they had to crawl toward their destination? There was no traffic at all. He was just going slowly because he liked to talk so much. He didn't want to get to the hotel because when he did, he would have to let his cohorts in conversation out of the van, and he'd be stuck with silent Laura.

She tapped her fingers nervously on her lap. Blast him, and blast the snow! If only she could take the wheel, the others could talk to their hearts' content, and she would fly this pint-size bus to Hisega.

"What would have happened if a beautiful woman had asked you for a date tonight? Who would have driven this bus?" the male passenger asked the driver. Everybody except Laura laughed. The man who had asked the question turned to look at Laura. He was grinning, and the grin seemed to be saying, "Come on, join in the fun! It's New Year's Eve!"

Laura smiled at him weakly. The driver answered the question by saying that a beautiful woman had asked him for a date. She was his wife, and he'd turned her down because he had bills to pay.

The word "date" sank deeply into Laura's mind. A New Year's Eve date. Sure. Everybody had one. She hadn't thought of the possibility before, but why hadn't she? Was it unreasonable to think that Michael would have a date

51

tonight? No, it wasn't. While she was rushing to him and praying that she would be in his arms at the stroke of midnight, he might already have the warmth of eager arms around him.

Laura realized that if her new and burgeoning fear proved true, Michael could not be faulted for being with another woman. Legally married or not, he had lived without the love and companionship of his wife for the better part of a year. And he was all man.

She huddled into her winter white merino wool wrap coat and dipped her chin further into the lush shawl collar of bleached white Norwegian fox. She clenched her ungloved cold hands on her lap. The heater was on, but it certainly wasn't doing the job it was intended for. Laura's feet were ice-cold, too. Her mind could not rid itself of the new image of Michael's spending this evening with another woman, and her heart seemed to be turning cold as the van crawled along.

Was Michael's New Year's Eve date that "somebody very special" he had said he went climbing with? Besides climbing, what else did they do together? *Stop it,* she cried to her darkening thoughts. She told herself that this was fantasy; in all likelihood there was not another woman. If the "somebody very special" was a woman Michael was attracted to, Laura was sure he wouldn't have mentioned her. She was probably just a friend. One of those ruddy and rugged outdoor types that look sturdy in flannel shirts and faded jeans.

Which is what I'll probably be wearing soon if I stay here, Laura suddenly thought.

If I stay here, she repeated to herself. That she might not stay was something she hadn't even considered before this moment. But if Michael did have another woman in his life . . .

The thought trailed off because another had taken hold in Laura's mind. He *might* have a woman in his home. Tonight. This moment. Oh, Lord.

She dwelt on it. *Oh, terrific. I arrive, with my cold little blue hands and cold little blue feet and big blue suitcases. I ring the bell. Yoo-hoo! Here I am! Happy New Year, darling!*

And Happy New Year to you, too, Mrs. Daniels. Mr. Daniels has an exquisite creature, whose hands and feet and heart are *very* warm, in his arms. On his knees. Maybe in his bed.

"You still cold, ma'am?" the driver asked, looking at Laura in his rearview mirror. Laura realized she had shivered out loud. "Sure wish I had a pair of my wife's gloves handy for you to put on. May I give you mine?"

"No, thank you. I'm fine really," she answered.

After what seemed to Laura like an interminable ride they finally arrived at the modest but proud-looking old hotel. After that they drove west out of town and through miles and miles of countryside. Lights became few and far between. The road was flat for a brief distance and then coursed voluptuously through the hills.

"Not long now," the driver said. He didn't talk much to Laura anymore. She realized this was because she was so unresponsive to conversation. She was sorry about that, but she just couldn't engage in chitchat. Her emotions were a never-settling flurry, much like the snow that maddeningly slowed their travel speed.

"How long'll you be visiting for?"

She was so lost in thought when he asked the question she wasn't sure for a moment that she'd been addressed. Then she looked up at the rearview mirror and saw him looking at her.

"I'm not visiting." As she said the words, she prayed

53

that they were true. "I'll be living in Hisega, with my husband."

He didn't disguise his surprise. The very silence seemed laced with skepticism.

"Are you surprised?" Laura asked abruptly.

"You bet. You sure don't look like someone who'd live here. But welcome to South Dakota. Hope you'll like it. Me, I wouldn't live anywhere else in the world."

Neither will my husband, Laura thought. She sat back as he turned off onto a road on their left.

"This is it. Hisega. A sweet place to live. Wish I was so lucky. Go right out your front door and catch your trout for dinner."

The road dipped and turned, becoming rougher as they drove.

"Hold on 'cause we might bounce," the driver told her.

Laura saw a number of log cabins, all of a fair size and a certain rough grace, and a couple of larger buildings that appeared to be empty. The driver explained that the buildings were kept closed in the winter, to conserve energy. The van crossed a small bridge and then another. As they approached Hisega, Laura's heart began to pound. *Oh, Michael, be here! Be alone. Be glad to see me. I've disappointed you, darling, but let me make up for it.*

They were slowly traveling the last brief distance when the driver asked, "Your husband already here in Hisega?"

"Yes," Laura said softly.

"What's his name? Maybe I know him."

"Michael Daniels." She said the words almost absentmindedly. There was absolutely nothing this man could say that would distract her thoughts now. She was here, unexpected and scared. Would she find that she was also unwelcome?

"Well, I'll be. I didn't even know Michael was married.

54

If he said so, I sure didn't catch it. Michael's a friend of mine. A swell guy. I really admire him. Everyone who knows him does."

Laura was shocked and distracted. She knew Michael wasn't a snob, but she was surprised to think of his being the friend of a man like this.

At the same time that she felt shocked, she also felt a little ashamed of her estimation of the driver. Who was she to say that owning an airport transport service in a small city wasn't an achievement? The Airport Limo might provide him with a better living than Michael's shop—The Ornery Ore—provided Michael.

On the other hand, Michael had disliked being with people who talked incessantly. This man loved to talk and was still chattering on.

But Laura wasn't listening. She was getting out of the van and was torn between conflicting desires. One was to proceed calmly, and the other was to leap up the steps to Michael's cabin, calling his name.

"Don't rush even if you're in a hurry," the driver said. "You don't want to slip and fall now."

Laura smiled, in gratitude for the man's concern, but she wanted him to leave quickly. This reunion with Michael had to be private. The light was on inside the cabin; therefore, Michael was home. He must be busy, or he would have heard the van stop and come to the window to see who was outside. But then he wasn't expecting anyone. So why should he look to see who it was? she thought.

Especially if he was entertaining a female guest. Laura shuddered with increased apprehension but squared her shoulders and prepared to take command of the situation. If there were a woman in the cabin, she would just kick her out. Right now she had to get rid of the driver. "Please put the suitcases down here, at the bottom of the steps," she said as she took her pearl gray wallet out of her darker gray alligator clutch bag.

"Let me carry them up for you. No sense in Michael having to do it."

"No, thank you. I'd rather you didn't. Thanks very much for a pleasant ride, and have a Happy New Year."

The man looked perplexed but did as Laura asked. "Say hi to Michael for me. You two have a Happy New Year, too," he said as he got back into the van.

She waited until he had backed up and turned the van around before she went up the steps. It seemed to take him forever. Laura was afraid that Michael would open the cabin door and that the driver would see him. The driver would not be able to resist stopping the van, getting out, and engaging Michael in conversation. Soon the three of them might even end up inside the cabin together. If that happened, Laura didn't think she would be able to bear the disappointment.

But at last the van was gone from sight. She was alone—and freezing to death. The snow was light, but Laura had stood outside long enough for it to cover her collar and her hair. She looked up at the sky, giving a few flakes of snow an excuse to perch on her nose for a moment before continuing their downward journey. Well, it was time to climb those steps. She felt as if she were two people, not one. There was a jubilant Laura Daniels who wanted to fly up the steps and pound on the door and be in Michael's arms before he realized what was happening to him. Then there was another Laura Daniels, who was scared to death. She was scared that Michael might not forgive her. *He came back to Beverly Hills to get me,* she thought, *and after we had made love, I turned my back and walked out on him. Our anniversary night was my second chance to be his wife. I may not be granted a third.*

Of course, if she stood outside his house much longer, she wouldn't need to worry about whether she would be welcome inside it. As her teeth chattered, she muttered, "Okay. Onward!" She lifted her smallest piece of luggage by its ice-cold handle and walked resolutely up the steps.

There was no doorbell to ring, but there was a knocker on the door. She used it. The dark metal her chilled hand gripped was colder than the leather-covered handle in her other hand. There was no response to the knock. She tried again, knocking harder this time.

He's not here! she screamed inwardly. *Oh, Happy New Year, Laura! You're stranded on Michael's doorstep in the middle of a snowstorm. You were too shortsighted to realize this could happen and too stupid even to think of wearing gloves.*

She bit her lower lip, then knocked a third time. At the same time she used the knocker she let the suitcase drop. In her misery she didn't care if it slid down the steps. She grabbed the doorknob with both hands, not because she expected it to turn but in a gesture of frustration.

The doorknob turned. Laura's lips parted in surprise. She opened the door tentatively and walked inside. "Michael?" she called softly, sensing as she did that no one was there.

At least she was in out of the cold. That alone was a blessing. But as delicious as the warmth of the cabin was, she knew she had to go back outside to get her suitcases. It took two difficult trips for her to lug them up the steps. Then she closed the door on the snowy night and stood in the stillness of Michael's home.

It was lovely, she thought as she looked around her. No, it was more than lovely. It was wonderful. The cozy rustic living room made her sigh. "Michael . . . darling, it's perfect!" she said out loud.

57

Rich wood tones were complemented by the deep gray of the slate hearthstone. A fire had been lit tonight, but only an occasional crackling ember was left to testify to its existence. But even without a bright fire the room was gently welcoming. The draperies, an ottoman's covering, and two throws on the flax-colored sofa were in various shades of muted earth tones. A bright orange rug and an orange and white afghan added vibrant color to the room.

The blanket looked very enticing to Laura. She was still freezing, but she took the wool coat off after a few seconds because she suspected it had absorbed the chill of the outdoors and was preventing the room's warmth from fully benefiting her. She had on an angora-blend white boatneck sweater with silver mesh detail at its neckline and a white wool skirt. Her knee-high boots of crushed gray leather seemed about as insulating as a handkerchief wrapped around each of her feet.

Laura had dressed carefully for the trip, choosing a delicate gold and jade bracelet and simple pearl earrings for her jewelry. She had wanted so much to look just right for Michael. But Michael wasn't here.

She stepped around the coffee table, which had a basket filled with ore samples on it, to get the blanket. She had it wrapped around her shoulders in another second. Ah, that was better, she thought. She snuggled into its weighty warmth and relished how it hung down all around her like an oversize shawl.

Then, with a little of the chill out of her bones, Laura decided to look at the other rooms. The decision made her feel awkward, and she hesitated, but finally, she headed for the dining room and sighed an appreciative "Oh!" when she saw it. In the middle of a round table of old pine was a lazy Susan, at the center of which was an earthenware bowl filled with fruit. The high slatted-back chairs might have been austere-looking if they hadn't been cushioned in the same warm earth tones that had been used so effectively in the living room.

Laura ran her hand along the top of a chair, thinking as she did that she would cherish having her morning coffee in this room. She looked up. Plate racks that ran the length of two walls, beneath the wide-beamed ceiling, displayed an array of what Laura was certain was authentic Indian pottery.

Laura smiled to herself as she fondled the chair top again. *I'm falling in love with Michael's home just the way I did last time,* she thought. When she first entered his Beverly Hills residence to do research for a magazine article, she had been enraptured. That house, though, had had every luxury lavished on it. This one hadn't. It was a simple house, and not very big. It certainly didn't have maid's quarters or five bathrooms. You could not have a party for many people in it. No, it was an intimate environment, to be enjoyed by guests who were there because you truly cared for them.

I love it! I love it more than the house in Beverly Hills, she thought.

The realization was a relief to Laura because she was sure the house in Beverly Hills would soon be up for sale.

Laura glanced all around the dining room again. *What did I expect?* she asked herself. *A dull cave? A shack? Michael wanted to live the way he thought real people live. Shouldn't I have realized that real people in Hisega have good taste and love their homes as much as people in Beverly Hills do?*

She turned to go into the kitchen, fully expecting it to delight her as much as the two rooms she had already seen.

It was cheerful and attractive, but it was not as tidy as the other rooms. And it did not delight her, not after she

59

had noticed that two of almost everything had been stacked on the yellow ceramic tile counter or placed inside the sink. The dishes from tonight's dinner had been scraped but not washed. There were two dinner plates, two bread and butter plates, two wooden salad bowls.

Laura liked the dishes. They were just right for the ambience of the dining room, but she wished she had a hammer so she could smash them. She also felt like breaking the two tall glasses that had been used at dinner tonight. They were lovely glasses; sort of early American in style, but she couldn't bear the thought of another woman's drinking out of them. The flatware was contemporary, she noticed, and realized she couldn't have chosen better herself.

Then she saw the coffee mug. It was half-hidden by a saucepan.

Only one mug had been used. Michael *always* had coffee after dinner, so his guest evidently didn't like coffee. But she liked to express her feelings toward a man in a way that left no room for misinterpretation. The mug that Michael had drunk from was of a kind that could be found anywhere. White, with black lettering, it proclaimed: "I love Michael." A bloodred heart substituted for the word "love."

Laura picked it up in hands that were suddenly shaking. She stared at it unbelievingly for a moment, and then somehow the mug slipped out of her hand. It fell to the floor with a loud crash, sending bits of broken pottery flying in all directions.

CHAPTER FIVE

Kneeling to pick up the broken pieces of the ceramic mug, Laura could barely restrain her tears. *I don't know what to do! I've made a horrible mistake in coming here,* she thought, feeling more miserable than she ever had before.

She went back to the living room after cleaning up the mess she'd made. She had to sit down and think. Holding the afghan tightly around her, she eased slowly into an armchair as if her body had suddenly aged and stiffened. She felt so weary. Hadn't it been a hundred years ago, not this afternoon, that she had left California?

The chair she sat in faced the sofa. Laura could picture Michael and his lover sitting cozily on that sofa. They probably had sat there tonight, before dinner.

She put a hand over her face and closed her eyes to blot out the ugly picture. *Oh, God, what did I do by coming here?*

It wasn't just that she had come to South Dakota. She had closed her studio. She had said good-bye to friends, some of whom had cried. She had asked her widowed mother, "Mom, will you be all right without me?"

Her mother, with eyes brimming, had answered, "As long as I know you'll be happy with your husband in South Dakota, then I'll do just fine."

Laura had hugged her mother, and they both gave up trying to hold the tears back. She said, "I know, Mom.

Don't worry about me. Whatever I find there, I'll learn to love and be grateful for."

She hadn't thought of this possibility, though. She took her hand from her face and stared at the sofa. *What are my options now?* she asked herself. *I can call a cab to come all the way out here to get me. I can walk quietly into the woods and freeze to death. I can be sitting here wrapped in an afghan like an old granny when Michael—or when Michael and his girl friend—return. Or I can keep busy by washing the damned lousy dirty dishes, and when they return, I can offer to turn down the bedcovers for them. Or . . .*

Laura got up from the chair, took the blanket from her shoulders, and flung it hard at the sofa.

Or I can be in bed. It's my *husband's bed, and if someone else has plans about sharing it with him tonight, she'll have to fight me for the privilege.*

Her stride had no reluctance in it as she went from the living room to the bedroom. This, too, was more than a nominally attractive room, but Laura was in no mood to appreciate its appeal. For all she knew, some of the decorator touches in this cozy little house weren't Michael's touches.

Almost involuntarily she sniffed to pick up the scent of perfume if there was any. There wasn't, thank God. Laura wasn't sure what she would have done if there had been.

She yanked the bedcovers back and glared at the pillowcases. Good. Neither had lipstick marks. She bent forward and sniffed. No feminine aroma, just the faint but delicious hint of masculinity. That was a relief; at least she wouldn't have to change the linen while she stewed and waited for Michael.

She ran her fingertips over the pillow. The sheets and pillowcases were flannel. The bed would be warm, warm and smelling of Michael. At least something was going right for her.

She went back to the living room to get her suitcases. She wasn't going to bother with unpacking, and she had no intention of putting on a nightgown, but she would put a few dabs of Michael's favorite perfume here and there. Especially there.

After placing the suitcases in a corner of the room, where Michael was not likely to trip over them and break his unfaithful neck, Laura went to the bathroom to wash up. This house did not have an elegant master bedroom suite equipped with a dressing room, mirrored wardrobe doors, a sitting-room retreat, and an onyx marble oval Roman tub with six "unwinder" jets. It had a modest bedroom and a modest bathroom, and they were separated from each other by a short hall. She went into the bathroom and found the light switch.

Even with the sconce lights at either side of the oak-framed mirrored cabinet, the room was not bright. But Laura assessed its contents immediately.

Two hand towels. Two washcloths. Two bath towels. The washcloths and bath towels were still damp. Michael had bathed before going out; perhaps his guest had, too.

There were two toothbrushes in the toothbrush holder. Laura could tell which one was Michael's. He always used the kind with longer bristles in the outside rows and shorter bristles in the middle. His was blue. The other was yellow. For an instant Laura considered rubbing the bristles of the yellow toothbrush on the bar of soap in a soap dish.

She didn't. It wouldn't have made her feel any better. Nothing would.

But she was not bowing out of this love triangle without a fight. She went back to the bedroom and got into bed.

The soft flannel sheets were comforting, and there was no chill when she got into bed even though she was nude. It was lovely. Laura hadn't known flannel sheets existed except for baby cribs. *This is something that won't require getting used to,* she thought as she snuggled down under the sheet and comforter.

She remembered that she had meant to put perfume on. The shock of seeing the extra towels and toothbrush in the bathroom had made her forget. But she wouldn't get out of this deliciously warm bed for perfume. She lay there, moving one foot back and forth to savor the softness of the flannel beneath and above it. She thought about Michael, remembering how desperately she had wanted to be in his strong, loving arms when the clock struck twelve and lovers everywhere whispered, "Happy New Year," to each other.

She turned her head to be able to see the alarm clock on the small round table beside the bed. It was 12:40. Someone else had given Michael his New Year's kiss. Don't cry! Laura told herself sternly as the thought caused her eyes to fill with tears.

Then, with the sounds of a vehicle stopping outside the cabin, Laura's mind was emptied of thought. For a long moment it was as if her spirit as well as her body were without motion. She held her breath without realizing it.

The front door was opened and then shut. For endless seconds she heard no other sound from the front of the cabin.

Laura's mind snapped back into high gear as she remembered that she had not found the door locked when she arrived and that she had not locked it after entering the house. This could be someone other than Michael, somebody who knew that Michael might leave the door unlocked.

Then there were footsteps, and Laura breathed a sigh. She could never mistake Michael's walk; she knew his walk as well as she knew his scent. And her relief was unutterably heightened by the realization that he was alone. No steps had preceded his; none echoed them.

When she heard the sound of water running, she realized Michael had walked to the kitchen. He was getting a drink of water. Laura could imagine him standing in front of the sink. He would set the glass down, look at the dirty dishes on the counter and in the sink, and groan inwardly at the thought of having to wash them in the morning.

Would he notice that the mug was missing? There was no time to worry about it because when he slaked his thirst, he would come into the bedroom. And when he did, he would surely turn the light on.

Impulsively Laura threw the covers off. If she were going to be Michael's New Year's surprise, she might as well surprise the socks right off his feet.

The newness of being uncovered caused a tantalizing chill to spread over Laura's body, but she knew it was more than the sudden exposure to cool air that caused her nipples to become taut. She was glad that had happened. Michael loved to see her when she was aroused.

Then she heard other, disturbing sounds from the kitchen. She couldn't believe what her ears told her was happening there. *He's doing the dishes!*

She made her hands into fists and pounded them on the bed, at her sides. *Oh, Michael, leave the dishes! I'll do them in the morning.*

It was too cold to remain uncovered while Michael washed, rinsed, dried, and put away dishes. She sat up and pulled the covers around her. The warmth didn't alter her state of desire, though. The slight friction of the flannel sheet on her breasts made them yearn even more to be caressed.

But not by hands that had earlier caressed another woman, not by lips that had kissed another woman.

Laura could not forget the evidence she had seen in the kitchen, the evidence that Michael was in the process of erasing. Nor could she forget the extra towels and extra toothbrush in the bathroom.

And the other evidence—that of her presence here? Had Michael opened the covered plastic kitchen trash container yet? Or, as he washed the dishes, had he begun to sense that something was missing?

I've just altered my entire future, Laura thought. *I've given up my home, friends, and career. This was to have been the most romantic night of my life. I'm lying nude in Michael's bed, alone, dwelling on the importance of a broken, cheap coffee mug.*

She waited. And waited. After what seemed enough time for Michael to have cleaned the kitchen of a thriving restaurant, he was evidently finished. Laura heard him leave the kitchen and walk to the hall leading to the bedroom. The wait was over. He would find her here in one more moment.

Love me, Michael, she screamed to herself. *Want me here. Keep me with you. Love me as if we'd never been apart.*

He went into the bathroom, closing the door behind him.

Laura sighed. She considered removing the covers again but decided against it. It was just too cold to continue to lie here uncovered, waiting for him.

The bathroom door opened. Michael came into the bedroom but didn't use the switch for the wall lamps that were on either side of the pine four-poster bed.

He put his keys on the bureau next to the door.

Laura could remain silent no longer. Barely whispering, she informed him of her presence. "Michael. Michael, I'm here."

"What the—"

He whirled to face her after snapping the terse words.

"I'm sorry if I gave you a start, darling."

"A start? You nearly gave me a premature death!"

If he was thrilled that she was here, it didn't show in his tone of voice. Sudden light in the room, when Michael turned the lamps on, made Laura close her eyes. When she opened them, Michael was leaning over her, with one knee on the edge of the double bed and his fists pushing deeply into the down comforter on either side of her.

Her nostrils involuntarily widened as she smelled his clean masculine scent. But because of the way he was pushing down on the bed with his fists, the covers were a restraint over her upper body. She couldn't move. The restraint wasn't pleasant. Her eyes were welling up with tears, and she wanted to brush at them with her hand. It would be a small favor for him to move his fists so she could have the use of her hand, but the furious look on his face suggested that it was not the right moment to ask him for a small favor.

His eyes were burning into hers. His mouth was a thin line. His nostrils flared, but not to take in the scent of his wife. His breathing was harsh. She could see the rage in his eyes.

Laura didn't need more evidence. She expected the anger to spill out of him in words, but Michael didn't speak.

Somebody had to. She swallowed hard, then said, "Happy New Year."

"You have a cold heart, Laura, if you just dropped in to celebrate New Year's Eve. I suppose you think of this as repayment for our anniversary. Well, you can forget it. You might as well get out of my bed and on the next flight back to California."

Laura did not turn her face from this fury. Her arms were restrained by the position of his fists on the covers, but she could have turned her head from his verbal assault. She didn't.

"I have—I have *needed* you, Laura! I have been insane with needing you! Loneliness for you has been eating my guts out!"

"And I've needed you, Michael." Laura echoed his words. "I've come to stay." The rage was all his; the sadness, hers. His words were scathing, hers were tender.

"Loneliness has been eating at my heart and soul," she whispered, "loneliness for you."

He stood up, then threw the covers off her.

Instinctively Laura wanted to cover herself up again. The eyes staring down at her body sought not to warm her with adoration but to chill her with scorn.

She didn't cover herself. Finally, though, she had to turn away from Michael's brutal stare. It hurt too much.

"Look at me," he ordered fiercely after she had turned her head on the pillow.

She didn't. It was all she could do to keep from crying. Looking at Michael's smoldering eyes would surely cause her tears to flow.

He leaned down over her again and took her chin in his hand. He made her turn to face him.

And Laura felt relief when he did because he had not touched her roughly. If anything, his hand was gentle. The tenderness of this touch was the only thing that was sweet, the only thing welcoming her.

But even with the relief she could not look at his eyes. She looked at his body instead. He certainly hadn't been out tripping the light fantastic on this New Year's Eve—unless he had gone dancing wearing a chamois cloth shirt and jeans, she realized with a newfound joy.

Laura breathed deeply, slowly looking up into Michael's eyes. She said his name in a whisper and then reached out her hand to place it tenderly on his thigh.

Michael gasped. He put his hand over hers, to press it harder against himself. "Laura . . ." he rasped once, and his eyes seemed to be melting from the burning pain of his love. He dropped to his knees at the side of the bed. He brought her hand to his lips and lavished urgent kisses on both sides of it.

Laura, turning so she could caress his bowed head with her other hand, thought—but could not be sure—that she had heard him sob.

CHAPTER SIX

Michael climbed on top of Laura and smothered her breasts with kisses while her hands raked through his hair ceaselessly. He kissed her sensitive nipples with increasing fervor until at last he heard her say breathlessly, "Michael . . . Michael. No more. Please."

He moved his head from her breasts abruptly. "Did I hurt you, angel? I'm sorry. I—"

"No . . . oh, no, my darling. I just can't bear this much desire."

He stared at her, then muttered that if he wasn't hurting her, he saw no reason to stop. She didn't argue, and he began to kiss her again. But these kisses were different. They were tender and loving. He coaxed each nipple with deliberate strokes of his tongue. He wanted to raise Laura's desire to a level where it would have to burst within her. She arched her back, and he thought, *Yes, Laura. Let it build up in you. Let it burst through your lips in moans of ecstasy. Lust for me, Laura.*

And she did moan. She also breathed words of love and need and desire. *I will show you what desire is, Laura,* Michael thought, and he almost sobbed again.

Desire. He had lain awake last night thinking of Laura. Desire had so overwhelmed him that he had finally leaped out of bed. He had thrown on some sweats and a parka, pulled boots on without bothering first about socks, and gone for a walk. It had been two thirty when he left, three thirty when he got back and gloomily slugged down a glass of brandy. It was excellent brandy, meant for long, slow enjoyment. He had poured it down his throat with as much civility as a runner gulps water at the end of a race.

Desire? Sometimes, when he got up in the morning, he went right to the chest of drawers where he kept a picture of Laura. The picture was underneath a pair of black socks, in the right front corner of the top drawer. He would pull the drawer out hard but reach for the picture gently because he was afraid of damaging it. It was a picture he had taken of her in the spring, before their parting. She had been walking in their rose garden, and he had caught her unaware. Now, in the mornings, he would tenderly take this picture in his hands and sit down on the end of the bed and gaze long and hard at it.

And he would know, then, what desire was.

Desire was an aching need, a hollowness inside, a painful constriction in the throat.

He would slip the picture back into its place beneath the socks and prepare himself to face another day of raw loneliness.

When he did that—took the picture of Laura out of the drawer and looked at it—he tried not to think about the key. The key was in the far right-hand corner of the same drawer.

It was the key to the house in Beverly Hills. He had been sure, when he replaced it in its corner after the futile trip to California on their wedding anniversary, that he would never use it again. Yet he could not throw it out. Nor could he touch it. If he ever used it again, he might break down and go back to the spoiled rich man's life he had walked away from.

71

Or he might throw the key at the wall and then, with his bare hands, break the chest of drawers down into kindling.

So he never touched the key. He would put the picture of Laura back in its place, try not to think about the key, and close the drawer slowly.

That, Laura, is desire, he thought.

He thought of the key now. Something had made it flash through his mind. He got up. When he moved away from her, Laura said, "Don't go! I'll bear all the desire you want me to feel for as long as you want me to feel it. Darling, stay with me."

"Just a moment, Laura. I want you to see what the word 'desire' means in this house."

He held the key up for her to see. "It's the key to our house. It's my symbol of desire. I've gone to bed every night knowing the key was here, in this room. Every morning I woke up knowing that it was here and that I was never going to use it again. I couldn't throw it out. I couldn't use it. And that was what desire meant for me. Desire meant hell—pure, unadulterated hell. And look at this little thing, Laura. It's just an innocuous piece of metal. But my God, its existence caused me pain."

Laura swiftly got up from the bed. "Let me have that," she said.

Michael loosened his hold on the key so she could take it from him. As she slipped it out of his hand with her thumb and forefinger, he noticed, for the ten thousandth time since he'd met Laura, that her hand was slender and smooth, with painted perfect nails. Classy, elegant, and oh, so kissable—that small hand.

Laura crossed the room to the window seat, where she'd placed her purse. She brought the gray alligator clutch to the bed and opened it. Seeing the purse triggered a memory. Laura had bought it the last time they had shopped together.

Michael remembered whistling to himself because of its price, and an odd thought had crossed his mind at the moment he looked at the purse's price tag.

Do women in Kansas spend money like that on a purse? he had wondered. *Or would they think that what Laura is doing—and what I'm being an accessory to—is insanity?*

He'd had the thought but hadn't mentioned it to Laura. And when she asked him, "Do you really like it?" he'd said, "Sure. It's very nice."

While they finished their shopping on North Rodeo Drive, he'd felt an envy of men who lived in Kansas or Montana. Men who had to do their shopping at Sears, Roebuck. Later he had wondered if those men envied people like him, and he doubted strongly that they did. But strangely enough, he found he envied them. Their lives were real. They did not have to validate their existence by buying seven-hundred-dollar suits at Michael Daniels. Their wives did not need alligator clutch bags that cost what someone might pay for a minor surgical procedure.

The afternoon of shopping he had realized much later had been one small step on his way to leaving California.

Laura removed her house key from a metal ring that dangled from an oval of brass with the Mercedes-Benz logo. She held both keys—his and hers—up for him to see. Then she walked out of the room.

Although curious, Michael didn't follow her. He heard the door open. He heard it close. He heard Laura run in quick, short steps back to the bedroom.

"Brrr . . . it's freezing out!" She shivered in his arms.

He gathered her naked warmth to his roughly clothed body and cherished having her face snuggled into the protective haven of his throat. Laura had always loved to do that, and although it tickled his throat, he loved her to do it.

"Did you throw both keys out in the snow?" he asked, laughing and rubbing her back and buttocks to warm her.

"Yes! As far as I could! Nobody will ever find them!"

The movement of her soft lips tickled him when she spoke and when she shivered, and she burrowed deeper into his embrace.

"I gave my spare key and Luisa's key to my mother. Now neither of us has one, Michael. And we'll never need one again."

Laura moved away from his body just far enough for her to be able to look up at his eyes.

Michael looked down at her eyelashes. They were so beautiful, so long and lush and mysterious in their perfection. Laura reached her arms up so both hands could entwine themselves in his hair. She knew he loved it. Her hands in his hair just above the back of his neck; her belly cozy against his pelvis, her face tilted upward and her eyes looking into his with pure adoration. *World, Happy New Year! At long last,* she thought, feeling more contented than she had in many months.

"I'm here to stay, Michael. Forever and ever. If you want me."

"If I want you? Does this feel as if I might possibly not want you?"

He moved sensually against her while caressing her back with loving hands. He kissed her several times, letting tenderness flame slowly into passion. He loved her deeply, fiercely but then remembered that he was still clothed. His jeans and shirt might be rough against her, so he eased back about a fraction of an inch. Then he kissed her again.

After the lingering kiss Laura said, "I know that you want me right now, darling. But I don't know if you

74

wanted somebody else earlier tonight. And I don't know who you'll want tomorrow. I pray it will be me."

He didn't know what in the devil she was getting at. Somebody else? "It will be you," he said slowly. "There's never been anyone else for me but you."

"Michael, darling, I don't *blame* you. You've been alone and painfully lonely. I—I know there was someone here earlier because I saw the dishes in the sink. Dishes for two. And I saw the mug she gave you, Michael. I broke it. I was holding it, and my hands started to shake. It fell. It wasn't on purpose."

"The 'I love Michael' mug?" he asked. "You broke that?" He felt a twinge of regret. The mug was a trophy of sorts. He thought quickly that he wouldn't be able to replace it tomorrow, the first of the year being a holiday, but he would get one the following morning if at all possible.

"I just felt so shocked when I saw it. Anyhow, that mug and the dishes for two and the second toothbrush in the bathroom—those told me the story. Not the whole story because I don't know the end of it yet. At the end of the story who is loved by Michael Daniels?"

Both of you, he thought. He held Laura close so she couldn't see the smile that he was trying to suppress without much success. "Laura Daniels," he murmured, stroking the honeyed apricot hair. "Laura Daniels is loved by Michael Daniels."

He would tell her all about her only rival in the morning. He didn't want to talk about another person now. Laura was here with him, and nobody else need be, not even in conversation. In fact, he wanted to end their conversation as quickly as possible.

"I wanted so much to be in your arms at the stroke of midnight," Laura said. "I wanted to make the plane go faster. Then, on the way to Hisega, I felt that the driver

75

was torturing me by driving so slowly. And when I got here and you weren't home, I felt like crying."

"Shh." He kissed her. Then he kissed her again. Her arms were around his neck, and he reached up to take one beautiful hand and bring it down between their two yearning bodies. He pressed it against himself, knowing that would convince her the time for talking was over.

The ploy didn't work. She rubbed him with an eager hand, but her words were just as eager. "Michael, I want to talk about her. I have to know—"

"There's nothing for you to know. You're not going to talk about anything." He scooped her up in his arms, kissed her gently, and set her on the bed. He put one knee on the bed and began to kiss her tenderly between her breasts. Then he kissed her navel. Then he pressed his lips to the triangle of gently curling hair. He nuzzled her there a long time. Then he began getting out of his clothes.

"Michael, turn back the clock."

He looked quizzically at her as he stepped out of his jeans.

"Please, make it be before midnight. Just for you and me. I don't care what time it is for the rest of the world. I want the New Year to begin when we're holding each other. And we'll look at the clock and count the seconds until midnight. Is that too silly?"

He picked up the alarm clock and began to reset it. "It's not silly at all," he said indulgently.

"Wait . . . before you do that. Tell me one thing, Michael."

He couldn't help smiling at her. She could be so whimsical and sentimental. He liked the idea of their having their own private midnight. It was nice; it was the sort of thing only Laura would think of.

76

"I know you don't want to talk about it, but I have to ask. Just tell me, please, before we make love . . ."

Her words trailed off. "What?" he asked. "Speak now, or forever hold your peace, woman. And if not forever, at least hold it for an hour."

"I will. Just tell me . . ." She swallowed. "Michael . . ."

She stopped again. Her words were like those of stage-struck actors who are terrified of coming out under the lights. "Laura!" he cried in exasperation. *"Talk,* or open your arms to me. Do something!"

"Tell me if you were with another woman tonight. I couldn't *bear* it if you made love to me after being . . ."

The look on his face must have been stern enough to shame her. She stopped talking again, but this time not out of hesitancy to confront him. "Oh, Michael, I'm sorry," she said softly. "You wouldn't do that to me ever. And I should have known it."

"You certainly should have known it." He finished resetting the clock, so that midnight would arrive in forty-five minutes. He set the clock on the table, got on the bed, and knelt astride Laura.

"Are you disappointed in me?" she asked.

"Of course not."

"Why aren't you disappointed?" she asked, and Michael found himself looking at a smile that turned him into a worshiping puppy before her. He'd first seen that smile when she came to his Beverly Hills home to write a magazine article. Six years later the smile had the same effect on him.

He eased himself down over her so his yearning desire could be felt by her smooth, taut belly. Gently caressing her, he murmured, "I'm not disappointed in you because you happen to be the most dazzling, the most wonderful, the most desirable woman in the world. And the sweetest to boot. Touch me, Laura. Hold me."

She did. Thirty-eight minutes later, when she was lying on top of him, he cautioned her to turn her head and look at the clock.

They looked at it together. In silence they counted down the minutes, then the seconds. Then they kissed. It was midnight, the start of a new year and a new life. Michael whispered, "Happy New Year, darling. I love you."

And Laura said the same.

CHAPTER SEVEN

Laura awakened to bright light streaming into the bedroom through windows covered with frost. She was immediately aware of having slept through most of her first morning in South Dakota.

Then she noticed that Michael had not slept through the morning. Wearing a red wool shirt, jeans, and boots, he was sitting on the white-cushioned window seat. He had opened the blue and white birch-patterned curtains and then sat down to watch as daylight gently coaxed Laura awake.

The raw wood-planked room was cheery with sunshine and bright colors. "I opened one of your suitcases and took your robe and slippers out, so you wouldn't be cold going from here to the bathroom," Michael said, indicating with a nod that her iced pink velvet terry robe was draped over the chair next to the bedside table. Laura saw that her matching slippers were on the blue rag rug beside the bed.

She sat up and stretched her arms luxuriously, then whipped her head from side to side so that her hair swirled around her face. After that she tucked her chin down to her chest and tossed her head back as far as it would go.

"You still do that." Michael laughed. "I always thought it was a nutty way for someone to start the day. The first time I saw you do it I wondered that you didn't get a crick in your beautiful neck."

"It keeps me from getting a crick in my neck. Mmm, darling, do I smell coffee? Do I see frost outside? Oh, Michael, it looks as if diamonds were ground to dust and sprinkled all over the world. I love your shirt, honey, and your boots. Have I told you I love the way you dress here? You're my rugged mountain man. Did I tell you how much I love your—*our* home? I wouldn't change a thing in it! How did you know I've always wanted a window seat where I could look out on a frosted winter landscape? And I'm crazy about the dining room. The Indian pottery on the plate racks is wonderful! Is it all hand-thrown?"

She stopped. Michael was both staring and laughing at her; his eyes were gleaming with total merriment. His arms were folded across his chest. Where the shirt-sleeves gapped slightly above the cuffs, Laura could see the dark soft hairs on his lightly tanned arms.

"I love the cabin, the frost outside, the smell of coffee, and the hair on your arms!" she cried happily. "I can just see a little bit of your arms. It's a good thing my vision is perfect or I wouldn't be able to enjoy looking at that tiny bit of you from this distance. I'd have to be content with seeing your face and hands. They're beautiful, too. Did you sleep as soundly as I did, darling? I didn't even dream until right before I woke up, and then I was dreaming we were walking in the snow without clothes on, and we weren't cold."

He was laughing harder now and shaking his head in mock dismay as she chattered on.

"I *know.*" She sighed. "Do you think I'll ever be able to stop?"

"If there were money riding on it, I'd have to bet against," Michael said. "But don't try to stop talking. I'm enjoying it immensely."

Now Laura was laughing, too. When she stopped, she

murmured, "You're looking at me with so much love. I hope you can see all the love that I'm feeling, too."

"I can."

For a few moments there was silence between them, but even in their silence they communicated on a level too deep for words.

Laura spoke first. "If you don't have other plans, would you show me all around today? Could we see Mount Rushmore and go to The Ornery Ore? I'm dying to see your shop. And would you build a snowman with me? And could we light a fire in the fireplace and have hot chocolate in front of it?"

He got up and came to the bed. When he sat down and put his arms around her, she rested her head on his chest and ran a hand lovingly along the muscles of his arm. "I really can't help talking so much," she said. "I think of one thing to say or ask you, and another pops out of my mouth right after it."

"Don't apologize. Your voice is the first music I've heard in a long, long time."

She lifted her head from his chest so she could look at his eyes. "Is that a line you give all the ladies who wake up in your bed at eleven in the morning?" She asked the question playfully, but the thought of another woman reasserted itself in her mind.

"Only the ladies with turquoise eyes and only if I have a burning desire to fix them a New Year's Day brunch. How about this, Laura? You take your shower, and I'll make the bed. You unpack, and I'll cook. Then we'll do all those other things you wanted to do. But do you really want to build a snowman? That's work."

"Oh, yes! With a carrot nose, and—what do you have in the refrigerator that would be good for his eyes?"

"Black olives?"

"Black olive eyes, and if you have an apple, we'll make the mouth out of apple slices."

"Sounds good. I'll slice the apple while you build the snowman's body. Is that fair division of labor?" Michael dipped his head down to kiss her shoulder while she laughingly told him how unfair she thought it was. She said they would each do an equal amount of work if he could lend her a pair of gloves.

"Didn't you bring gloves to South Dakota?" he asked, taking both her hands in his.

"No. I was so crazy with wanting to be with you I didn't think of gloves. It's a wonder I did anything right. I might have forgotten to bring shoes. Michael, your mentioning gloves reminds me of something."

She told him about the man who had driven her to Hisega from the airport, about how he had kindly offered to let her wear his gloves. "He said you're a friend of his. I was supposed to say hi to you for him."

"We are friends. That's just like Clem to offer his gloves on a freezing cold night. He'd give you the shirt off his back."

"I didn't think the part about your being friends was plausible," Laura said.

Michael frowned slightly. "Why?" he asked.

"Because he couldn't stop talking. And you aren't overly fond of people who run off at the—"

She stopped herself. Michael was grinning, and she could see that he was just barely able to restrain his laughter. She beat him to it and enjoyed a good laugh at herself. "I don't know what's gotten into me today," she cried. "I just want to talk and *talk* to you. Michael . . ." She paused to kiss him on the chin. "Michael, I've *been* talking to you, day and night, since I got in my car and left you in the house on that horrible morning. I've been talking to you in my mind even when I was watching movies, working at my desk, or trying to pay attention to clients. I talked to you when I lay awake at night and when I got up in the morning and in the shower. Especially in the shower. Didn't you ever hear me?"

"I wish I had," he murmured, and he brought her in closer, enfolding her naked body in arms that smelled faintly of newly chopped wood. "I wish I had," he said again. "Then I wouldn't have been so lonely."

"One day I forgot myself and talked to you out loud. I was meeting a client for lunch at the Beverly Center. When I got to the restaurant, she wasn't there yet. So I was waiting, and all of a sudden I realized I had said, 'Michael, darling, I know we will be together again someday,' out loud."

Michael chuckled, asking, "Are you sure? Maybe you just thought you'd said it out loud."

"Oh, no, I did. The hostess was standing near me, and she said, 'That's right, honey. You *will* be together again. I have faith that we'll all meet our loved ones in heaven.' "

Michael laughed with pure pleasure.

I can still make him laugh, Laura thought happily. *I'll make him laugh and smile and feel good, so often, he'll forget the sadness of those months of separation.*

"Go take your shower," he said when he'd stopped laughing. "And don't stay in there talking to yourself too long. We've got to get this day moving, or the snowman will never materialize. You can't trust snow in the Black Hills. It's here, and then it's gone."

"Okay, but first tell me about your friend Clem."

"Well, to begin with, he would have to be on a roll to chatter as much as you're chattering this morning. Other than that, honey, he's a guy I know from Big Brothers."

"Big Brothers?"

"Of America."

"Oh, sure, I've heard of that organization. Are you somebody's Big Brother?"

"Yep. I have been for five months. As a matter of fact, it was because of Clem that I got involved. He came into The Ornery Ore with his Little Brother, and we talked a bit. He suggested I stop by the Big Brothers headquarters in Rapid City the next time I was in town. I did. A few days later I met Joe Kills Deer."

"Your Little Brother?"

"Yep."

"He's an Indian boy?" Laura asked and suddenly became very thoughtful.

"Yes. He's full-blooded Sioux."

"Michael," Laura said very slowly, "did Joe Kills Deer have dinner here last night? And take a shower?"

"He sure did. Then we went to two New Year's Eve parties. One at another Big Brother's home, and one at Joe's Cub Scout leader's home. Fortunately both places were in the same neighborhood. It's called Robbinsdale. Then I dropped Joe off at his aunt's, in North Rapid City. He lives with her and her kids. Then I drove slowly back to Hisega, expecting nothing more than dirty dishes to be waiting for me."

"Oh, Michael. Michael, I love you. When I saw the dishes and silverware in twos and the toothbrush, I thought . . ."

"I know what you thought. You have a wicked mind because of the fast crowd you hang around with in Beverly Hills."

"Not anymore I don't." She kissed his wonderfully masculine, newly shaven chin. It was just like Michael to get up early in the morning no matter how late he'd stayed up the night before. Laura calculated that they couldn't have fallen asleep before three, and it had probably been well after that. "Have you been out chopping wood already?" she asked. "You smell like wood."

"Yes, ma'am. And I shoveled snow."

"While I slept in. Let me make brunch for you, Michael. You relax and I'll . . . oh *no!* I just realized the mug I broke must be from Joe."

"Yes, but don't worry about it. We'll replace it. He stayed over with me a few days of Christmas vacation, but since he'll be back in school tomorrow, he won't be over here for a while."

"Oh, I hope we can find one like it. Was it his Christmas present to you?"

"No, my birthday present. He gave me the mug and a God's eye. He made the God's eye as a Scout project. God's eyes are Indian symbols, made by winding yarn around sticks. They can be magnificent or modest. I've got Joe's, which is modest, hanging in the shop. And he baked me a cake, and that was kind of touching because Joe's diabetic—severely diabetic. He couldn't eat any of it."

Listening to this, Laura thought of how Michael's last birthday had affected her. She had been miserable. Close friends, guessing that this would happen, had insisted she have dinner at their home. She had picked at the food on her plate and tried to make interesting conversation. Nobody mentioned that it was Michael's birthday. Laura had gone home from that dinner exhausted, drained. In bed she had prayed that Michael, too, had spent the evening with friends.

Now, knowing that Michael had spent his birthday with a very special friend, Laura felt grateful to the boy. She suspected that Joe had unknowingly been diminishing Michael's loneliness for five months.

"Will I meet Joe today?" she asked. "Can we go over to his aunt's?"

"No. I don't want to share you with him or anyone else today."

She felt a little relieved. It did not seem likely that Joe would hold her in high esteem.

"Does Joe know about me?" she asked.

"Yes. He'll be shy about meeting you because of what he knows."

Sure he will. He thinks I'm an ogre, Laura thought. *The Wicked Witch of the West, who wouldn't live with her husband and who didn't bake a cake for him on his birthday.*

It occurred to her then that she had never baked anything for Michael. Not cake, not pie, certainly not bread. When baked goods were called for, she went to one of a half dozen superb bakeries she frequented. Whatever baking had gone on in their home had been done by Luisa.

All I ever did was put his bread in the toaster, Laura thought.

"Joe thinks you're wonderful, something like a goddess. He's been hearing extremely biased descriptions of your virtues."

Laura couldn't imagine what those were. "You should have told him I never baked you a pie or a cake," she said with self-resentment.

"Oh, hush. You did a million wonderful things for me. Do I have to list them for you?"

"Yes, if you have a spare ten seconds. Talk slowly, and you won't have too many seconds left over."

Michael chuckled. "Ah, the throes of guilt," he said teasingly. "While you're doing this guilt number on your-self, I should probably take advantage of your sexy body. Who needs pies and cakes?"

"Oh, *do!* Take advantage of my body, Michael. I feel there's so much lost time to make up for."

He tweaked her nose instead and got up from the bed. "Not now. I want to feed you, show you Lake Pactola, which is just a few minutes from here, and then go to the shop and Mount Rushmore. Afterward we'll come back and build your snowman and sit by the fire, drinking cocoa. Then, if you still feel up to it, I'll take a little advantage of your body. Do you have something warm to wear before I do that?"

"Yes. Michael . . ."

Michael was already on his way out of the room. He turned and smiled when she said his name.

"Are you as happy as I am?" Laura asked tenderly.

His smile vanished, and he seemed to be carefully considering his answer. Speaking from where he stood in the doorway, instead of coming back to the bed to be near her, he said, "On our wedding day and on about two dozen fantastic occasions since then, I thought that life couldn't be any better than it was. But I was wrong. Last night and this morning have been better. Just sitting over there on the window seat, watching you while you slept, was better. Chopping wood while I knew you were in this house was better."

Then he came back to the bed and sat down. "You came to me, Laura. It beat your having married me. It beat your having crossed the Atlantic Ocean on a ship with me and our swimming off the shores of the Greek isles together. It even beat that incredible week in Tahiti. I guess I'm trying to tell you that your coming here to me, of your own accord, is the best thing that's happened in my life. Thank you, sweetheart."

Michael kissed the palms of both her hands and then touched his lips to hers in tender tribute.

"Now we know what you've done for me in the last twenty-four hours," Michael said huskily. "What can I do for you, besides having orange juice and coffee waiting when you get out of the shower?"

"Two eggs, sunny side up. One slice of toast, with jelly. Bacon, if you have it."

"You've got it, kid. I've put your towels in the bathroom. Give the water two minutes to heat up before you get under the shower."

He kissed her softly and was on his way to the kitchen.

CHAPTER EIGHT

At her first sight of the presidential faces sculpted in stone Laura's breath caught in her throat.

Michael chuckled. "Everybody does that the first time. Any American seeing Mount Rushmore for the first time without having a physical reaction wouldn't have any soul."

"Only the first time? You mean I won't gasp every time I see it?"

Michael pulled the red pickup into the empty large parking lot below the national monument. "No, but you won't yawn either. It looks as if we're the only ones here. Nothing will be open. The gift and art shops are closed during the winter, but we can walk up to the observation platform. This is when it's nicest to come here, when nobody else is around."

Flags of the states, in order of their admittance to the Union, lined the winding path leading up to the buildings and observation level.

Michael and Laura walked slowly, each with an arm around the other. Laura was wearing an all powder blue outfit of wool slacks, a crew-neck cashmere sweater, and a short-waisted suede jacket. Her casual wardrobe was not extensive, but she did own two pairs of walking shoes, and she'd had the good sense to bring both pairs with her to South Dakota. Today she was wearing one of them. She had declined Michael's offer of big thick fleece-lined black gloves but had promised she'd wear them when they built their snowman.

Since she wasn't wearing gloves, she kept one hand snuggled in her jacket pocket and the other in Michael's jeans pocket.

"Is your hand warm enough in there?" he asked, patting where it rested snugly against his firm narrow hip. "Wouldn't it be warmer inside your jacket pocket?"

"It would, but I like feeling your fanny. Look, there's the California flag."

Laura looked up at the simple brown bear aloft between the far more complex emblems of Wisconsin and Minnesota.

"Do you feel like saluting it?" Michael asked. He looked down at her seriously but then winked to show that he knew better.

"I'm a South Dakotan from now on," Laura said affirmatively. "Michael, stop." She stood still for a moment, staring up at the faces. In wonder she said, "I've seen pictures of this all my life, but I can't believe how really magnificent it is."

They climbed the flight of stairs to the observation platform. No one else was there. As they walked toward the waist-high wall at the platform's end, they gazed up at George Washington, Thomas Jefferson, Abraham Lincoln, and Theodore Roosevelt.

"Do you remember the sculptor's name from some long-forgotten social studies text?"

"Gutzon Borglum," Laura said without having to pause and think. "A few years ago there was talk about changing the name of the airport in Rapid City to the Gutzon Borglum Memorial Airport, but the idea didn't take hold."

Relishing the brief look of astonishment that played on

Michael's features, Laura refrained from giving away the secret to her formidable knowledge of local trivia. "Let's sit down," she said. "You were right about coming here first. I'm glad that we're seeing it while it's still bright out."

Laura had wanted to go straight to The Ornery Ore after they had their brunch and cleaned the kitchen, but Michael insisted that they see Mount Rushmore first. He wanted to make sure Laura saw the monument while the day was still sunny. January's days were short in this climate, he explained, and he didn't want her first sight of the sculpture to be grayed by dusk. When she protested that her real desire was to see his shop, he said, "No, because if I take you into the shop, I'll get carried away and insist on showing off every ore." So they entered tiny Keystone, a niche in the mountainous gateway to Mount Rushmore, drove right past The Ornery Ore, and in less than a minute drove west out of town.

Michael lifted Laura onto the platform wall, then sat close to her and held her hand in his, on his thigh. Their backs were to the monument, but the sculpture was clearly reflected in the huge windows of the building they faced. They had a perfect, if slightly eerie, view of it. "I want to know how Borglum did this," Laura said. "And how did he happen to come here to do it?"

"I know how and why, but right now I don't happen to care," Michael answered. "What I want to know, in depth, honey, is how *you* happened to come here."

"You already know. I'm married to a man who lives here. I love that man. I missed him, terribly. So I bought a plane ticket."

"I love the story so far, especially the part where you love the man. But give me details."

Laura had stopped concentrating on the reflection of the

91

sculpted mountain. She looked into Michael's eyes and tentatively asked, "Do you have to have the gory details?"

"Every one."

"I'd rather talk about Gutzon—"

"Laura."

"Okay. Where do I begin?"

"Three weeks and a day ago. We were in the kitchen. I'd had breakfast, and you hadn't. My chair was on the floor. You were wearing a blue dress. Luisa was probably eavesdropping on us, and you"—he pressed her hand against his thigh, squeezed it gently, and said—"you walked out."

"Yes. I walked out," Laura began.

"I went to my studio and worked all morning. I had no feeling, no emotion. I felt like a robot. Finally, I couldn't stand it anymore and called Zale Winters. I asked him if he wanted to have a late lunch.

"We met at André's, and, Michael, Zale was a real friend to me that afternoon. He made me laugh, something I thought I'd forgotten how to do. He didn't offer advice. He told me he didn't think it was his place to do so, but he was so supportive I just don't think I could have managed without him.

"That lunch was my last social engagement for four days."

"You went four days without seeing anyone?" Michael asked incredulously.

"Nobody except clients. Looking back on it, I think I was really with you. I spent all the time thinking about you, talking to you in my mind, and hoping. I hoped and hoped. Actually hope started when I got back to the studio after lunch with Zale. I convinced myself that it was possible you wouldn't have left—that I would get home and you would still be there. When I did get to the house and saw that the car you'd rented at the airport wasn't in the driveway, I felt like kicking myself for entertaining false hope all afternoon. I sat on the edge of our bed and tore the nightgown—the one you'd ripped the night before—into satin rags. And I cried. Anyhow, by the time I went to bed that night I was entertaining another false hope."

"What was that, honey?"

Laura hesitated, wondering if she was wise to go into all this with Michael. Giving voice to her reluctance, she said, "Oh, Michael, I don't want to tell you. I just wasn't thinking straight."

"I know the feeling," he said softly. "So you hoped you were pregnant?"

Laura stared up at him in astonishment.

"I carried that in my beggar's cup, too, for about two weeks," Michael commented with a wry smile. "Then I asked myself, 'What makes you think a pregnant mule would be less of a mule than a nonpregnant mule?' "

"Thanks. I needed that."

He shrugged, grinned at her, and kissed her hair. Laura watched all this in the reflective glass.

"The mule wouldn't have been less of a mule," she admitted with a sigh. "I thought that if I were pregnant, I'd get *you* back, that you'd return to California and stay. And be happy. Michael, I built the hope of pregnancy up until it was reality in my mind. Then, when I learned I wasn't pregnant, I was devastated. I carried on with my work, but emotionally I felt as if I'd suffered a real loss. It was hysteria, I guess."

"No, it was real loss. Dashed hope always is."

She turned and leaned her face against his arm. "Thanks. Thanks for understanding. Well, I started to work—and play—even harder. Harder than I ever had. I put in more hours with more people than I ever had before. I was on the go constantly, trying to squeeze two days

93

into one. I was never alone. I started one working day with a seven thirty breakfast meeting and ended it after midnight, when a client chose a crewelwork tapestry fabric over plain burgundy silk for her living room. By then I was a zombie. The client—Delta Haggerty—said, 'I know you're tired, Laura, but why don't we do the sitting-room retreat while you're here?' "

"And you didn't do it?"

"Unh-unh. I didn't even smile while saying a hasty good-bye."

"Sweetheart, you were on the way to liberation. You were on the way to South Dakota. You just didn't know it yet."

"I guess. When I got home that night, I didn't go inside right away. I walked in the rose garden. A few yellow roses were still in bloom, but all the other bushes were bare. I thought about . . . I remembered how you brought that rose to California, and caressed me with it. I thought about living in a place where there really are four seasons, where nothing blooms in winter. Does anything bloom here in winter?"

She turned her head and looked up at his face as she asked the question.

"I hadn't thought so, until I watched you wake up this morning. When did you know, honey? When did you consciously know that you were coming to me?"

"Four days ago. I was at a pseudomansion in Bel Air that a couple named Porter recently bought. I was with Mrs. Porter in the living room, a depot-size room that nobody is ever going to use, and all of a sudden I just didn't care. Michael, that room was beautiful. Exquisite. It had a marble hearth and . . . never mind. I'll spare you the description, but that room, even barren, was an aristocrat among rooms. There was so much that could have been done with it, and the Porters cared nothing about expense. I was being given a free hand with their money, with the understanding that whatever I did would be fine as long as the living room emerged obviously posher and more elegant than the other living rooms in the neighborhood. But I just clicked off. I didn't even understand what I was doing there. Mrs. Porter said, 'Would you put a grand piano in that corner, Laura? Or by that window, for the light? No one will play it, of course, so light doesn't matter. We can just stick it in that corner for effect.' Michael, she looked at me to hear what I would say, and I said, 'Mrs. Porter, I don't care where you put a grand piano that nobody will play. Why don't you balance it on your head?' "

Laura sighed. She still felt bad about this incident. It had been the first time that she behaved unprofessionally as a designer.

"Thanks for not laughing at that," she said, looking into Michael's eyes. Then she considered why he wasn't laughing. He was probably a bit disgusted by her lack of professionalism. Michael had always believed that people who faltered professionally did not care about their work, the people they worked for, or the people who worked for them. He'd fired salespeople for being rude to customers.

"Are you disappointed in me, honey?" she asked, prompting the chastisement she felt she deserved.

"Yep. I am. I think you missed a great opportunity."

Laura was surprised and looked at him blankly. Finally she ventured to say, "If I'd stayed until the house was finished, we wouldn't be sitting on this wall together, Michael. I thought you'd be disappointed because I was rude, not because I left California without finishing a job."

"That's not what I meant. Of course, I'm glad that you didn't stay. I'm overjoyed. I just think you missed an opportunity to deliver a classic line. See, when she asked where she should stick the grand piano, you should have said, 'Madam, why don't you—' ' "

Laura stopped him right there. "Michael, what I *did* say was bad enough! What you're suggesting would have ruined my reputation."

"Not with me, it wouldn't have. Go on. What happened after you left? I assume Mrs. Porter showed you the door immediately."

"She did, and I wasn't even embarrassed or ashamed. I was just a big emotional blank. I walked out of the mansion envisioning you in your cabin, in some secluded little place called Hisega. I felt faint with the desire to be there. I longed for you so badly I couldn't start the car right away. Well, I had lunch with my mother awhile later, and I couldn't pay attention to anything she was saying. I could see her mouth moving; I could hear the sounds of her words. But that was all. I felt stifled, claustrophobic. Mother realized something was happening to me and asked what was wrong. I didn't answer. She got worried, asked again, and put her hand over mine. Then I broke down. I cried and cried and ruined lunch for heaven knows how many people. I probably entertained a few others. It was funny in a way. Mother ended up paying for food we hadn't eaten, and we left. Mother said she's never going back there."

This time Michael did laugh, and Laura joined him. "Here comes the really bad part," Laura said. "Are you sure you want to hear it?"

"Here comes Zale Winters," Michael replied quietly.

"Yes. He's a good man, Michael."

"I don't doubt it. He's a good writer, too. What happened?"

"I recuperated from the trauma at lunch and kept a

dinner engagement with Zale. We stopped at a party first, and it was more of the same. People talking to me and my not hearing. But since it was cocktail party talk, it really didn't matter. Then we went to the restaurant. I complimented Zale on the new suit he was wearing. When he joked that the prices at Michael Daniels had gone up since the new management took over, I snapped at him."

Laura noticed a frown cross Michael's face when she mentioned the company's new ownership. Did it bother him? Was there a twinge of regret? She doubted it and went on with the rest of her story.

"I asked Zale not to mention the name Michael Daniels again that evening, and I asked it in a curt tone. I just was not behaving like myself, and Zale picked up on it."

"We were at the Excelsior. You know it, Michael. It's that elegant new restaurant on North Rodeo Drive. Anyway, Zale told me just what I needed to hear. He made me see things just a little more clearly. He told me that the separation was taking its toll on me, both physically and emotionally, and he made me realize that I had to do something about straightening out my life.

"I thought he was going to tell me to go to South Dakota to be with you, but he didn't. He surprised me. He told me that perhaps, since we had been separated for more than half a year, it was time for me to consider divorce; to begin to build a new life was the way he put it. He also told me that he wanted to be the one to give me the happiness I deserved.

"I felt awful, as if I had somehow taken unfair advantage of this thoroughly decent man. For the first time I realized that by having lunch or dinner with Zale, I was encouraging him to think we might have some kind of future together. I guess the platonic relationship had been platonic only on my side."

"What did you tell him?" Michael asked, his voice low and grim.

She looked into his eyes, her gaze one of reassurance, before she went on.

"I told him there was only one man in the world for me," she said simply. "And I'd been keeping myself estranged from that man for much too long. I told him there was only one decision possible for me at this point, and that was to go to South Dakota. So all my unhappiness ended at that moment, Michael. Right there, just before my hearts of romaine salad was served, I got rid of the pain. I was almost giddy while we had our dinner. Fortunately my exhilaration was infectious. By the time we split a baked Alaska even Zale seemed excited that I was going to South Dakota. When I got home, I could hardly wait for morning, to make the arrangements that would get me from there to here. Oh, the Harrises were thrilled to snatch Luisa up, and they took Mouser, too."

Michael jumped down from the wall and stood in front of her. He gently spread her knees apart so he could stand between them. "You gave away my cat? The only cat that ever liked me? The one that purred whenever I came near it?"

"I did! What are you going to do about it?" Laura laughed. She was utterly relieved that Michael saw fit to comment on Mouser's fate rather than on Zale's.

"Why, I'm going to elicit a few purrs from you by doing this."

After pulling a glove off, he laid his hand against her face. His fingers and palm had been kept warm by the fleece-lined glove, and Laura's cheek was cold. Laura turned her face into the toasty oven of his hand and purred.

"And this," Michael murmured, using his other hand,

98

which was still gloved, to find a breast that was snuggled behind its own warm covering of suede jacket, cashmere sweater, and lacy bra. Even though the massaging fingers and palm were heavily wrapped, and the breast was well covered, Michael's caresses stirred a gentle flame.

"Michael, you shouldn't. Not here."

He was massaging both breasts now, and his lips grazed the fine line of her smooth, slender jaw. "Why not here? Nobody's looking."

"You're wrong. The Father of Our Country and the Great Emancipator are looking. So are Jefferson and Roosevelt."

"But Jefferson was a lusty soul, and Roosevelt said to kiss softly while carrying a big stick. So that's what I'm doing."

At Michael's perversion of Roosevelt's words Laura couldn't help laughing. She grabbed his hands and pulled them from her breasts.

He put them back and massaged with more seductive conviction. At the same time he began to play with her lips with flicks of his warm, moist tongue. He would dampen the soft contours of her slightly parted lips quickly, and the cold mountain air would dry them just as quickly. "Darling, no!" she begged. In response he moved his ungloved hand to a thigh that was firmly sheathed by soft wool over a satiny lining. He trailed seemingly casual but knowing fingers along her thigh's inner curve until he found the taut seam where the pants leg met its mate.

"Michael, *stop!*"

"Shh. Enjoy it. It's so good. If it feels this good now, Laura, think how it will feel when your pants are off. Just close your eyes, breathe the crystal mountain air, and imagine that."

"I'm not taking my pants off out here!" Laura gasped between short, steaming breaths of crystal mountain air.

Michael's lips grazed over hers several more times before he asked, "Why not, my love?"

His finger continued to stroke her with slow, firm movements, but when he brought his hand up firmly over her abdomen, Laura knew his desire was unquestionable. More than six months of starvation had left a reservoir of hunger deep within Laura. She wanted Michael to be inside her, beneath where his hand was gently massaging. She wanted it as much as he wanted to be there. But she could not go through with this. What if a family of tourists surprised them in the act? What if a ranger came by?

"I can't do this, Michael! It's not right!" Her protests were whispered, but they rang with urgency as he slipped a finger behind the waistband of her slacks.

"It's right, and it's wonderful. I'll keep your back to the monument, angel. The presidents will see only your sweet little behind."

"Michael, that's—that's *awful*. Oh, I wish you'd stop."

It wasn't true, and she knew he knew it. Her desire for him was so strong now that she could never quell it.

"Laura, I always loved this about you, the way you respond to me. Sometimes, in a crowded room, I thought I'd aroused you just by catching your eye."

"Sometimes you did."

"And here we are. This isn't a crowded room. Show me your passion, Laura. Let's give this place a new meaning that just you and I will know about. We'll make it a shrine to our love."

Laura shook her head slowly. "Oh, Michael, you're mad. You're a crazy person. Honey, a guard will come. A ranger. Whatever they have up here. We'll be arrested. We'll be infamous."

100

"I don't care."

"Our names will be in the paper."

"I don't care. Love me now. Right now!"

"No one will go to your shop, ever again. The Ornery Ore will be finished."

"I'll take the risk. Come closer. Put your hand on me."

"No one will hire me as a decorator! I'll be washed up here before I even get started!"

"Wonderful. The scenario is getting better and better." He had slipped her sweater up, and Laura had the odd experience of being fondled by one warm hand and one cool glove.

"The Big Brothers . . . *Joe will know!*"

His hands tightened against her flesh. Then he let her go. They both were breathing hard. "You hit me in a very vulnerable area," Michael said accusingly.

"Thank God! But I'll make up for it, darling. Let's go to The Ornery Ore now. We can be there in a few minutes."

Michael was still standing between her spread knees. He shifted his stance and ran his ungloved hand through his thick thatch of tousled hair in exasperation. Laura, seeing the undiminished swelling of desire against his jeans, almost laughed.

"I feel like a desperate teen-ager." Michael grimaced. "I don't think I feel like opening the shop and showing it off to you. I'd rather sulk because I didn't get my way. Who cares about gems?"

"*I* care about gems," Laura murmured after she'd wound one arm around Michael's neck and inserted her other hand where his thighs met. She did to Michael what he had done to her earlier, moving her fingers in exploratory strokes along the taut fabric of his jeans. She smiled when passion made him shudder and groan hoarsely against her hair.

101

"Come on, teen-ager. I vote that we go to The Ornery Ore so you can try to sell me your most precious gems."

"Do you think you'll buy?" he asked huskily, raining kisses on her face.

"Whatever you have to offer, I'll buy," she answered with a gentle squeeze of her hand.

"Eric, don't run! Your shoelace is untied!"

Michael quickly set Laura on her feet when the maternal warning interrupted their loveplay.

"Daddy, will you tie my shoelace?"

"Sure thing, big fella."

Laura, two steps away from Michael now and with her hands tucked demurely into her jacket pockets, looked at him gleefully as she silently mouthed, "I told you so!"

"Oh, Lord, remind me always to listen to you," Michael muttered. They walked down the steps to the path, and when they turned toward the parking lot, they passed the young family of three. Michael said, "Hello! Happy New Year!"

The sentiment was echoed by three adult voices and a child's wide-eyed stare.

CHAPTER NINE

Just as Michael had predicted before they left Hisega for the afternoon outing, he got carried away with showing off everything in his shop to Laura.

She didn't mind; she was enthralled. She had never been inside a rock shop before. In spite of her knowledge of Michael's exquisite taste, she had half expected something tacky. *Wouldn't a rock and mineral shop have dusty hunks of rock piled on top of each other in dark corners?* she had wondered. *Wouldn't baskets be filled with worthless stones for tourists to buy at twenty-five cents apiece?*

The Ornery Ore was not like that at all. Tiffany's could not have displayed its wares with more pride and taste than Michael displayed his. Each ore was given enough space in the shop to have visual effectiveness. As in an art museum, everything was labeled. In some instances brief typewritten paragraphs described items on display. Laura was reading the description of arsenopyrite, a silverish mineral that was tarnished brown in parts and streaked gray-black. The commentary said that when struck, it smelled like garlic.

"That's nicknamed mispickel, for some reason," Michael said when he saw Laura lingering over the arsenopyrite.

"Miss Pickle?"

"Well, not in two distinct words."

"Miss Pickle," Laura repeated. "I like that."

"You and Joe. It's his favorite. He hints once in a while that he'd like to have it."

"Then let's give it to him," Laura suggested. She wanted so much for Joe to like her and to be glad that she was here. She knew little about him except that he was an eleven-year-old Sioux who was diabetic, an orphan, and a rock climbing enthusiast. And that he loved Michael. She had only two things in common with all that: She had once been eleven, and she loved Michael. If Joe were anything like her at that age, the surest way to winning his confidence was to give him a gift.

"I give him very few gifts, Laura. Only on his birthday and Christmas so far."

"How come?"

"Partly because it isn't necessary. I give him my time and friendship and get his in return. I don't want him to expect gifts from me, to value the relationship because it brings him material things. Also, his aunt is poor. She works, but she doesn't make enough to give extras to the six kids in that house. If I give Joe gifts frequently, he'll be in danger of expecting more luxuries than he's usually going to get, and his cousins might start envying him—as well as resenting their mother for not buying them presents. And—"

"Oh, don't tell me any more," Laura interrupted. "It's so depressing. All your reasons make sense, but now I want to buy him an electric train set, a horse, a soccer ball, and a bike. Ten-speed and very expensive."

Michael chuckled lightly. "I know. That's exactly what I usually feel like doing, in spite of everything I just told you. I'm crazy about that kid. For Christmas I got him a pair of boots, but I longed to buy all those things you mentioned. He has a bike, but it's in sorry condition.

Honey, he wouldn't have anyplace to put a train set or keep a horse. But he has a horse in a way. When he spends weekends in Hisega, he takes care of Misty."

Laura made a quick mental tour of the little house in Hisega. No, there was no room for a train set. Nor was the terrain in Hisega conducive to bike riding, so she couldn't suggest their buying a gleaming new ten-speed bike and keeping it for Joe to ride on weekends.

"Let me give him the piece of ore he wants," she said. "That couldn't possibly spoil him, cause envy in his cousins, or lead him to expect presents from you frequently." She hugged Michael's arm and smiled.

"Nope. I suspect Joe has a deeply rooted desire to take a hammer to this hunk of iron, arsenic, and sulfur. He wants to know just how much of a garlic odor he can exact of this rock by smashing it to smithereens."

Laura laughed. She gave up on the mineral for Joe for the moment and chose an exquisite specimen of violet-tinted dark blue lazurite for her mother. For the Harrises, who had an anniversary coming up, she selected a splendid piece of vivianite. The pearly green luster of the handsome mineral would find a home in either the Harrises' fir green den or emerald green solarium. She chose six more specimens to send to friends, putting the same care into each selection that she would if she had been shopping at Bonwit Teller.

"This is not exactly what I had in mind when I suggested we come here. I had thought we could try something more romantic than examine gems."

"Huh? Oh! Well, that can wait. These things are brand-new to me, and I'm fascinated by them."

"Keep breaking my heart. I can take it." He sighed. Then he suggested an olivine, with granular masses of olive

105

green and lime crystals, for another couple in Beverly Hills who were good friends.

"Picking minerals out to send to people is so lovely," Laura said. "It's like saying good-bye to friends a second time, and it gives them something very symbolic to remember us by."

"It's also depleting my stock," Michael said but without the least note of complaint in his tone. "Are you through? Pretty soon it will be too dark out to build a snowman."

"Can't we build one in the dark?"

"No." He laughed. "It just isn't done."

She was holding minerals in each hand, as he was, and she smiled. As he had claimed at Mount Rushmore, sometimes he could arouse her just by catching her eye. But he could also make joy well up in her with just a smile. The slight upward curve of his mouth and the humor in his gray eyes had just done that to her. She felt flooded by well-being. That did not, however, mean that she would refrain from building a snowman in the dark just because Michael Daniels said it wasn't done. She would build one right outside their bedroom window, where it could be seen from the window seat. That way she would be able to enjoy the carrot-nosed creation first thing tomorrow morning.

"Why isn't it done?" she demanded with a smile.

"Because children who build snowmen are supposed to be indoors having their dinner after dark, and interior designers who have just migrated from Beverly Hills are supposed to be inside also, loving their men. There won't be any tourists or minerals to distract us, and I am *not* going to listen to any reasons you might come up with to go outside. I didn't have your body beneath or on top of mine for half a year, Laura. You *owe* me."

"Forget the snowman," she said nearly in a whisper. "Let's take these and go home."

"Good thinking."

"Do you have a hammer at home?" she asked, making his brows rise in question.

"Sure."

"Good. I'm taking the arsenopyrite for Joe, and when he hits it with the hammer, I'll sniff the garlic with him. I want him to like me, Michael."

Michael's face broke into a grin, and he shook his head as if she were amusing but foolish. "Laura—Laura, my only love, you name one person on this lopsided planet who doesn't like you, and I'll throw in a horse with the arsenopyrite for Joe."

Her eyes went wide with happiness and victory as she cried, "Mrs. Porter, the lady with the grand piano balanced on her head!"

"I have to learn not to challenge you," Michael said. He put the minerals he was holding down on a glass counter top, slid open the door to another glass cabinet, and got the arsenopyrite out. "I always lose."

Dear Zale,

Your letter was a lovely surprise. I do apologize for not having written. I'm afraid I owe that apology to many good friends. What happens is that I think of writing to someone, to the point of practically writing the letter in my mind, but then I don't get it down on paper. And as time slips away, there is so much to add to the unwritten letter I start imagining it as a massive project. Well, so much for excuses. I just read your newsy letter and am answering immediately.

It did seem like a massive project, Laura thought as she looked at what she had just written. Perhaps she should just telephone Zale instead. But that would be the easy way out. Zale had typed a four-page single-spaced letter that was rich with news. It had been much more enjoyable to receive than a phone call would have been. She felt she must respond in kind instead of phoning, even though she knew that writing a long letter was easier for Zale than for most people.

But where should she start? By describing Hisega and the Black Hills of South Dakota? She wouldn't know where to begin. It was summer now; winter's philosophical beauty was past, as was the first real spring she had ever experienced. There had been heavy rain, inconvenient mud, and incredible rainbows. Now wild flowers dotted the emerald fields and pine forests with all the colors of a child's gaudy Easter basket.

The native and migratory birds couldn't rival the flowers for color but made up for that with their cacophony every day at dawn. The creek ran vigorously. Everything had the color of summer, the sounds of summer, and the smells and tastes of summer. Michael said that the best was yet to come; in August they would pick bucketfuls of the wild raspberries that grew near their home.

Laura sighed. It was probably best not to try to write a physical description of her new environment. It would take forever. Besides, Zale's being a writer intimidated her. He, no doubt, could make the Black Hills spring to life with written words, but she probably couldn't.

Should she write about her happiness with Michael? How they had been reunited and gone on with their life together without any remorse or recrimination over the months spent apart? No, of course not. Zale had mentioned two women he was seeing, but he was still alone.

She could no more write of her marital well-being to Zale than she could eat a hot fudge sundae in front of Joe.

That was it; she'd write about Joe.

Michael joined the Big Brothers of America when he moved here, and he has a little brother named Joe Kills Deer. Joe spends nearly every weekend with us, and we have decided to ask his aunt if it's all right for him to spend a few weeks of the summer here. Our house is small, so he sleeps in a sleeping bag in the dining room. He'll be here tonight, and tomorrow we're going to take the pontoon out on Lake Pactola. While Michael and Joe catch fish, I'll work on my column. More about that later.

I was a little scared of Joe at first, and he was timid with me. Children hadn't been a real part of my life—not since I was one—and I thought I'd say and do everything wrong. Also, I realized that from Joe's perspective I was a threat. He had been Michael's only "family" before I got here, and the two of them shared wonderful times together. During the winter Michael kept The Ornery Ore open only on weekends, so he had time to spare for Joe. Joe must have thought that all that would change when I got here. It didn't, of course. Do you know what, Zale? When I saw Michael and Joe together and realized how much they meant to each other and gave to each other, it made those months of separation seem worth it. The separation took on meaning because if Michael and I had come to the Black Hills at the same time, Michael probably wouldn't have become a Big Brother and met Joe.

Oh, we bought him a horse the first week I was here. He named it Spotty. Besides the fact that it has chestnut spots on an otherwise white fanny, Joe once had a neighbor who had a wonderful dog named Spotty. Joe loved the dog, hence the horse's name. Michael's horse is named Misty, and mine is—believe it or not—Miss Pickle. I won't elucidate because one explanation of how a horse got its name is enough for one day.

I don't ride often, as there isn't time. Usually I'm commuting to Rapid City in my big Chevy Blazer. The name of the game here is four-wheel drive. You don't see the kinds of cars that are *de rigueur* in Beverly Hills. Even in Rapid City there's very little traffic. I have to tell you a funny story. I have a client in Spearfish (that's a tiny college town about twenty minutes from Hisega) who is completely refurbishing a vintage home that's been in her family for four generations. Once when I went to see her, she looked frazzled, and she explained that she had just had to navigate Spearfish's downtown traffic at noon. "I'll never do *that* again," she cried, wiping her brow like a battle-weary soldier. I laughed and insisted that when I go to California on a visit, I'm going to take her with me and show her the Santa Monica Freeway at five in the afternoon or Westwood Boulevard on Friday night.

Laura went on in her letter to tell Zale that she was working four days a week as a decorator for a furniture store in Rapid City, that this summer she was teaching a course in interior design at a business college in Rapid City, and that she'd been asked to continue teaching the course in the fall.

110

But I've also been approached about teaching a night course at the air force base. I really do want to say yes to that and teach at both places, but the drive to the base would be just awful in winter weather. It's an hour each way. I'll probably decline. Offers like that excite me, though. I'm discovering that interior decoration, when you're working within a budget, is more of a challenge than when you're working without one. I think I love my work here even more than I did there. The best of it is that I've begun writing a decorator column for the paper. People write in questions—about everything from how to judge quality in furniture to how to remove a ketchup stain from a brand-new sofa—and I answer as best I can. It's a brief column, so I have room to handle only one question at a time. But I answer all the questions I get with personal letters. I think the column is unique, and I have to admit to having a fantasy of syndicating it. That's getting carried away, isn't it? Then again, I may have been inspired by your success story. I'm referring, of course, to your having pounded away at the typewriter keys for several years without selling anything and then rising to the very top.

Well, Zale, I could write on and on, now that I've put pen to paper. But as I said, we're having a special guest for the weekend. Sometimes Joe is here, and we have a date in town. He says he doesn't mind. His aunt's home is so crowded and noisy he likes the peace and quiet when we go out and leave him alone. He really is a dear person—a special part of our life.

Take care, Zale. Michael and I are looking forward to reading your new book as soon as it's released. When it becomes a best seller, I shall probably brag to people from Deadwood to Hot Springs that I know you. Michael sends his best.

Affectionately,
Laura

Laura reread the letter and decided it was satisfactory. She'd touched on practically everything, omitting, of course, her one source of unhappiness. But she couldn't confide to any friend that she was beginning to fear she had waited too long, that she would never have Michael's child. Michael never mentioned wanting a baby, never even hinted at it. But she knew. She had known in California, and she knew that now, with his life freed of so many stresses, he must want one even more.

She hadn't even told a doctor her fear. She had been meaning to go to one but had been afraid of what he might tell her. Would she ever be able to recover if he told her that there would never be a baby?

The door opened. Laura turned with a glad smile to see Michael come inside. He'd been gone only a short while, but that didn't matter. Every time he came into view she felt a wave of happiness wash over her. She would never get over that half year of separation—not entirely. It had left her with a special sense of appreciation when she saw Michael after so much as a few hours' absence. He stood beside her dining-room chair and gently pressed her head against him. A warm, rough hand that knew every inch of her body and was confident of its power over her caressed her throat and shoulder.

They didn't speak for a moment, just reveled in each other's presence. While Michael stroked Laura's shoulder, she lovingly moved her hand over his hip and thigh. She had a feeling of wonder in touching him, in knowing that he was hers to touch tonight, tomorrow, next week, and next year. *If you went half a year without seeing any sun in the sky or expecting to see it ever again, and then you had the sun back, you would practically worship its path across the heavens,* Laura thought. *That's how I feel when Michael comes home to me or I come home to him.*

"What has this gorgeous designer, teacher, and journalist been up to while I was gone?"

"I just finished answering a letter from Zale Winters. Do read his letter—it's funny. I think I might have told him more about an eleven-year-old boy, a horse named Spotty, and a decorating advice column than he could ever have wanted to know. Would you like to read it?"

"Not now. I left groceries in the truck, and I'd better get them and put them away."

"Did you get lettuce for Joe?" Laura asked. Joe, forbidden sweets because of his illness, had a passion for lettuce. Every night, before going to bed, he ate a whole head of iceberg lettuce while reading a book or watching television.

"Two nights' worth of it. Crazy kid. Sitting there with a head of lettuce and reading. He's like a literate rabbit." Michael chuckled at the fond image and idly trailed a finger around the curve of Laura's jaw. Then he rubbed her lower lip with his thumb. He did it a second time, and Laura maneuvered quickly—getting the tip of his thumb between her lips where she wanted it.

"Mm, I love you," she murmured when she was done kissing his thumb.

Unexpectedly she found herself eye to eye with Michael. He had dropped down to squat on his heels beside her chair.

"How much do you love me, Laura?"

She put her hands on his face and felt with reverence the hard and high cheekbones, the soft lips, the sculpted masculine jaw that only hours after having been shaved was

113

shadowed by virility. She brushed his hair off his forehead, not because she minded that it was always falling down to his irresistibly dark and handsome brow, but because she liked to touch it. "More than you know and more than I could ever express. Don't make me try to tell you how much, darling; it can't be done."

"I can think of a way for you to tell me. Words won't be necessary."

A smile began to play on Laura's face. If this were an invitation to make love, she would gladly accept.

"Have a baby for me, Laura. Complete our happiness."

Laura hoped the gut reaction she felt at his words wasn't showing on her face. Instinctively she felt that their lovemaking would not be the same from now on. It had been joyous and adventurous, sensual and playful. Now was it to become only a means to an end? And if the goal weren't reached soon, wouldn't any seductive teasing of each other's bodies become a farce? Wouldn't the ecstasy of passion fulfilled become hollow, possibly sad?

As these thoughts flitted across her mind, she saw Michael's look harden. The change in his features was almost imperceptible except for an upward movement of his strong jaw.

She brushed the hair from his forehead again. "I'd like that, too," she finally said.

He nodded, very slightly, and then in one fluid motion he was standing and looking down at her. "Sure you would."

"Michael . . . I *would!* I think about it. I—I just try not to become obsessed."

She had almost blurted out that she'd been trying to become pregnant. But the way he was behaving was making her feel defensive. She didn't like it. She *had* been trying to give him a child, without telling him in order to

114

spare him the worry she was feeling and to spare their lovemaking the strain that could sap it of its vitality. Now it seemed as if she were being punished for her pains.

"Nobody's becoming obsessed, Laura. I just thought that since we'd come this far in getting our lives sorted out, and since you're about to become thirty-two and I'm older than that, the time might be ripe for us to become a real family."

Her heart thudded as his words hit home. She gripped the edge of the table with white-knuckled fingers. She caught a quick glance at the large, flawless emerald-cut diamond on her left hand. It glinted with every color of the rainbow—every color of the hurt and fury rising in her. Swallowing the hurt and holding back the fury, she said in an even tone, "We are a family. You and I—together—are a family."

"Yes, well . . . in a way we are. But we're not a complete family yet. I think of a family as being parents and their offspring, and I would prefer to be part of that kind of family. If you wouldn't prefer it, I'm not going to force you."

Laura digested that carefully. Not force her? He had said once that he wouldn't force her to leave Beverly Hills, but he had forced her all right. He'd left her. He'd given her six months and three weeks of despair. He'd given her the choice of giving in to his will or dying a little bit every day of her life. Oh, yes, he had forced her.

In a quiet, even tone that didn't hold a hint of rancor Michael said, "I'd better get the groceries. Joe's lettuce has probably wilted."

He turned and began to walk away.

"Just a minute!"

Michael stayed with his back to her, even when the sound of her chair hitting the hardwood floor resounded in

115

the room. Laura was standing up, fuming, and ready to turn him around to face her by force if he didn't do it voluntarily.

Then he rounded on her. "You don't change, do you? You're a very spoiled little girl, Laura. Given half a reason, you'll have a tantrum—every time."

"I'm *not* having a tantrum."

"Your chair is on the floor. That smacks of a tantrum."

"It fell! As yours did in the not so distant past! Remember?"

"I do. Oh, yes. I remember your walking out on me very shortly after the chair fell."

"I shouldn't have done that. It was childish. But it was also the only thing I could think of to do. I wasn't ready yet to let you have your way."

"It wasn't a question of having my way. It was a question of which direction our lives were going to take. You were having a tantrum all that morning the way you're having one now, and that's why you took a hike."

"Michael. . . ."

Laura stopped talking after she said his name. She bent down and lifted the chair. When it was righted, she held tightly to its top, not knowing if she was holding it for support or so she would be able to lift it over her head and bring it down on Michael's skull the next time he said the word "tantrum."

"Michael, it *was* a question of which direction our lives were going to take, and it *was* a question of your getting your way. I'm not the only spoiled person in this room. You've always gotten your way. When you wanted money and success, you got money and success. When you wanted me, I was yours. When you wanted to uproot our lives, to walk away from success, or change direction—whatever you want to call it—I gave you your way. I made

116

you wait, and we both suffered, but ultimately it was your victory."

"It was your victory," Michael said very softly. "You must see by now how much leaving Beverly Hills has enriched you."

"I do see. I feel enriched. But you *made* me leave Beverly Hills. When I got here, you praised and thanked me for coming to you of my own accord. But it *wasn't* of my own accord. It wasn't at all. You forced me. I was dying without you."

"Do you miss Beverly Hills? Do you miss the phony sophistication and the—"

"Yes! *Yes yes yes! Sometimes I miss it very much!*"

She was shocked—easily as surprised by her vehement outburst as Michael was. She stood there with her mouth open and her chest heaving. Her breathing was hard, her temples pounded, and the unshed tears were scalding.

Michael was nodding slowly, as if understanding something unpleasant but unchangeable for the first time. His look was ice. Laura had noted once before—the morning after their last anniversary—that for hardness nothing rivaled a pair of green-flecked gray eyes blazing with contempt. She noted that again. And people said that diamond was a hard substance.

He didn't ask what she missed about Beverly Hills, but she chose to inform him anyway. "I miss my friends," she said. "I've known some of them since elementary school. I miss my beautiful home. I—"

"I should have taped how you gushed over this one when you got here!" he shot at her.

"Sure I did! I love this house! But it's small, and when Joe's here, it's crowded! Three people don't fit into this house comfortably, and there aren't enough closets! Pardon me if tripping over a soccer ball in the dining room

117

and almost falling facedown onto an electric train layout makes me miss my great big house!"

"Is Joe the problem, Laura? Don't you want him to be here—or is it just me?"

She was too angry even to speak. She just stood still and hated him. She'd had a few fights in her thirty-one years, but not in any of them had she been hit as hard below the belt as Michael had just hit her.

Their glares were locked for another moment, and then Michael turned.

"Don't leave this room," Laura commanded between clenched white teeth. Her mouth and throat were so dry it hurt to talk.

He faced her again, his arms folded across his chest. Although summer had just arrived, he was already tanned, and a dusting of dark hair deepened the tone of his bare arms. He wore a pewter knit shirt and new, unfaded jeans that in the low light of the wood-planked room looked nearly charcoal. He was a study in dourness, looking as if an ominous cloud capable of heartless destruction were waiting to burst inside him.

"You're awful," Laura said quietly. "How dare you accuse me of resenting Joe? I'm as good to him as you are. I care for him as much as you do. Maybe I love him more than you do. Your saying that we aren't a real family because there are no offspring shocked me. I feel as if Joe *is* our child and assumed you did, too."

"That's convenient."

"What?"

"Sure beats having a big belly, labor pains, and dirty diapers to contend with. Joe saved the day, huh?"

Laura felt herself go cold. When she raised her head so that her chin rested on the tips of her fingers, she said slowly, "Do you know, Michael, that right now I could kill

118

you? I won't because you'd interpret it as my having found another convenient way to get out of having your child."

"And to get back to Beverly Hills." He spit out the words derisively. "Any jury would empathize with your motive and let you go free. You were *forced* to give up the lush life of Southern California to live here in this godforsaken hellhole. The judge would wonder what took you so long. Do you want to do me in now, or should I get the groceries out of the truck first?"

"I just want to tell you what else I miss," she said. "Because I think there was more to living in Beverly Hills than expensive lunches. I think you have a shallow conception of what we left behind."

He shifted, shrugged, cocked his head to regard her more disdainfully, and said, "Educate me."

"Thank you. I miss my mother. Is that contemptible? I think it's a shame that in her old age she will see me very very seldom. I miss our rose garden and how you would go outside first thing in the morning and cut a rose for the breakfast table. Is that childish of me? Or maudlin? I miss going to exciting restaurants and stores, and I miss the culture. I miss the Hollywood Bowl, the Greek Theater, the Norton Simon Museum, the Los Angeles County Museum of Art, and the Music Center. I miss—"

"I think I've got the picture." He turned to walk out.

"Oh, no, you don't! Stay here because I'm just warming up, Michael."

Slowly he turned back to hear the rest. Laura ignored the look of anger turned weary in his eyes.

"I miss reading the *Los Angeles Times* in the morning and the *Herald-Examiner* in the evening despite the fact that neither of those papers would have been interested in my column. I miss the nearby places where we went for weekend vacations. Spearfish and Deadwood have their charms, but so did Santa Barbara and Palm Springs. And while we're at it, I miss the wonderful variety of fresh produce in the markets, and seeing the ocean, and . . . *and I miss everything! Everything!"*

"Then go back."

His cold tone and disinterested manner infuriated her. The fact that he could so nonchalantly tell her to leave after she had worked so hard and given up so much to be with him made her ache with sorrow and rage. Before she even knew what she was doing, she lunged out and grabbed him.

CHAPTER TEN

Seeing her fingers gripping Michael's arm shocked her. Instinctively she wanted to let go and see if the fierce grip had left marks on his flesh. She didn't, though, because it was more important to prevent his leaving the house. Her own roughness and the spoiling food, be damned. Something had been started here, and it needed finishing.

"Laura, let go of my arm." Michael's tone was an unmistakable indication of his fury. But he didn't try to throw her hand off, and his next words were spoken less menacingly. "I'm going outside to get the groceries. I've said all I'm going to say, Laura, and I'm not going to indulge one of your little tantrums."

Laura didn't let go, although her grip had lightened somewhat at his words.

"Laura, let go of me!" he demanded. "I'm just a rock shop proprietor now, remember? Spoiled groceries mean wasted money, and every dollar earned by a poor slob like me counts! Or are you planning on taking another job? Is there something to do with decorating that you can fit in between midnight and dawn?"

Laura's mouth fell open. She licked her lips. Then she let go of his arm. She noticed her fingers had made a slight mark, but she didn't care. "That was cruel," she said, her trembling voice a hoarse whisper. "Go put your groceries away. I'm sorry. . . ." Her voice nearly broke, but she managed to blurt the sentence out forcefully: "I'm sorry I detained you!"

"You're not going out," Michael informed her, guessing her intention as she left the living room.

"The hell I'm not!" she shouted. Her handbag was on the dresser in the bedroom, and she went for it. She'd gotten out of her straight-skirted dress and into a white chenille warm-up suit when she came home from work this afternoon and was too angry to stay in the cabin long enough to change into street clothes. She didn't know where she would go. Maybe Rushmore. Maybe one of the lakes. She wished she were near the ocean. If she were in Beverly Hills, she thought as she fished frantically for the keys in the bottom of her clutch bag, she would head out Sunset Boulevard. When she got to the beach, she would park the car and walk on the hard-packed sand until she dropped.

She reentered the living room, carrying her purse in one tensed hand and her keys in the other.

Michael was still standing where she'd left him. His hands were balled on his hips, and his jaw was tight. His legs were spread. He looked ready for combat. Incongruously he parted sternly set lips and said, "The fight's over. It's time to talk reasonably. Let's sit down together and hash everything out."

"Let's not!" Laura growled at him as she attempted to stride to the door.

He took two steps backward as she was going forward, his arm reaching out to hold her fast. Her momentum was so strong she could feel his arm muscles harden against her stomach. "Let me go!" she cried, pushing harder. If he actually did release her now, she might fall on her face, but she didn't stop straining. She didn't care if she fell; she didn't care if he sprained his arm; she didn't care if she had to check into a hotel wearing a warm-up suit and without any other belongings. She didn't care if the sky caved in on them or the world exploded. She just didn't care.

"I won't let you go out, Laura. It's not safe to drive when you're this angry. Come and sit down." Surprisingly his voice held a slight conciliatory tone. "Please," he added, sounding downright gentle. Too late. The gentleness somehow fueled her anger. She muttered that she could worry about her own safety. He said, "I love you. I don't want to fight with you." But she ignored his words and tried to break free of his hold.

"A few minutes ago *you* wanted to talk. You were right. We have to get everything off our chests," Michael argued.

"I was *wrong!* There's *nothing* to talk about. I don't have anything to get off my chest. The only thing I want off of me is your lousy arm, Michael!"

She hadn't looked at his face once since he had imprisoned her at his side. Now she looked. Meeting his eyes almost made her groan in bitter frustration because even when she hated him, he looked too wonderful to resist. Angry at herself for even thinking about how attractive he was, she tried to wrestle her way out of his iron grip. Turning her body as much as she could and trying to force him away by using her elbow, she didn't win freedom, but she managed to rip her top. The quick sound of tearing fabric made her stop her frenzied movements. Its effect on Michael was to make him let her go.

Laura looked down at where the top was torn on her right side. This outfit had been a quickly bought going-away gift from the Harrises, given to Laura during her hurried preparations to fly to be with her husband.

"I'm sorry," Michael said.

"Don't bother being sorry! You're good at tearing my clothing when you hold me against my will. I'm going to change. Please try not to rip what I put on because I'm going out!"

Since he'd apologized, she expected acceptance of just about anything she had to say. It wasn't so. He reached out again, this time to grab a fistful of white chenille that was draped over her stomach. He pulled her up close to his body and kept her there. She could feel his fist against her middle, and of necessity her legs pressed against his.

"I wasn't apologizing about the tear." He enunciated the words very slowly. "I didn't make it tear. You did. And this is the first time I've held you against your will, by the way. The other time, which you just referred to—our anniversary—you wanted me to hold you down on that bed. That time I tore your nightgown, but this time I didn't tear anything." He let go of her top, then added, "I was apologizing, Laura, for the ugly things I said. They *were* cruel. They were low-down, vicious, vile, and uncalled-for."

Laura stood silently, feeling her breathing calm down, getting her frenzied emotions under control and feeling her spirit climb up—slowly—from the pit of rage. Michael was silent, too. Laura smoothed the twisted chenille back into place. After a moment's pause she said, "I can stitch it up. It's right on the seam."

"Good," Michael said.

"Do you want help with the groceries?" she asked weakly.

"Yes, thanks. Here, let me put your purse away for you." It had dropped from her hand minutes before, and he stooped to retrieve it. He went with it to the bedroom. Laura waited for him to come back. He didn't. She walked slowly to their room. Michael was sitting on the edge of the bed, his head in his hands. She ached for him so much that her heart turned over. Wordlessly she put a hand against the side of his head, then ran her fingers through

124

his hair. He put his arms around her and pulled her close against his belly. "God, Laura, I don't know how I talked to you like that. I could cut my tongue out. Please believe that I didn't mean it, darling. Please, Laura."

With both hands in his hair, she told him she believed him.

"When I thought you were serious about going back to California, I felt I was drowning," Michael muttered against her. "I was drowning in my need of you, of us."

"You were drowning in your need for a baby," Laura said softly. "Michael, I knew you wanted a baby, but I didn't—I didn't dream your need was that great."

"It isn't. It isn't. I just need you."

"And I'm not here enough for you. I work too much of the time," she said sadly.

"No! I swear that's not what I really feel. Laura, I've been proud of your work here. In California you helped a lot of rich people spend their money. But here you help ordinary people make the most of what they have. Honey, I'm proud of your being a teacher, too, and I could bust my seams with pride in your column. Don't believe what I said out there. It was senseless." He raised his hands to her face and said, "You give to people, Laura. You're not a taker; you're a giver. I wouldn't change you."

She put her hands over his, then slid them down his arms. One of these beautifully sculpted loving arms had felt her bruising fingers on it; the other had felt her push against it with all her strength. "Honey, did I hurt you?" she asked. "This poor arm must ache from my pushing so hard."

"I was afraid I had hurt you," he said. "But I was impressed by your strength. You were beginning to feel as if you had a ton of weight to push with."

"I've been trying to gain weight. I want to weigh a ton."

125

She sighed, pulling his head back to her middle and burying her hands in his hair again.

"You what?" he asked, his hands tracing her slender curves.

"I want to weigh a ton. When you have a baby growing inside you, you gain weight. Or so it would seem. I've been trying for months. I didn't want to tell you."

"Laura, honey, why not?"

"Because it's sad. I'm beginning to think we can't, Michael. I didn't want to share that fear with you. But even more, I didn't want to ruin our lovemaking. When we make love to each other, it's perfect. I didn't want us to have that kind of tension—a task to perform when we were in each other's arms."

Michael shook his head as if clearing his mind. "Sit down," he said, and she sat on his lap. "How does your stomach feel?" he asked, gently rubbing it.

"Wonderful, now that you're doing that."

"Did I hurt you when I pulled you by the top?" He smoothed the fabric gently while asking the question.

"Unh-unh. Michael, all those California things I said I miss. I *don't* miss them all the time. Not even often."

"You sure?"

"I'm sure. Honey, once in a while I do miss certain aspects of our old life because it was a good life. In many ways it was wonderful."

"I didn't know you missed California, Laura. You never said a word."

"I never saw any reason to talk about it. Dwelling on what you can't have, or have left behind, just wears you down. I love it here, honey. I do. I'm happy."

"Positive?"

"Positive! I don't want to go back. Please don't ever tell me to again, even if we're in a fight."

126

He kissed her lips softly. "We'll get a bigger house," he said, before kissing her again.

When the second, longer kiss ended, Laura said, "I don't want to move away from Hisega."

"We won't. We'll find something out here. If we can't find a house that's right for us, we'll build one."

"Right away?" she asked with a certain trepidation. Already she was starting to miss this small jewel of a home. It was where her new life had taken form.

"Not right this minute," he said, cupping a breast with his hand and gently defining its curve with his thumb. "We're going to make love first, build a house second."

Laura sighed, feeling blessed because Michael was pleased with her again. They'd made up so thoroughly he could even joke with her. She knew he was doing it so she wouldn't worry about not being able to have a baby. When his assurances became more sensual than babying, though, she reluctantly reminded him of the neglected groceries.

"What groceries?" he asked.

"Mmm, Michael. Ooh, darling. The ones in the truck."

"What truck?" he murmured against her hair. "I don't see any truck. Did I ever tell you how cute you look in that outfit? Let me take it off your delicious body, so we can inspect the torn spot better."

"Michael, there's milk out there, and cottage cheese."

"There're more tasty treats than that right in here," he said. "Come on, Laura. Come on, baby. Don't think about anything except this. Nothing else matters."

But something did matter. "Michael, how can we? After what we've talked about? I'm so afraid that our desire to have a baby will ruin our lovemaking. Now that it's out in the open, it scares me to death."

"Stop worrying about it, and don't ever start to worry again."

"How can I help it, darling? I've had friends whose desire for babies consumed their whole lives. They—"

She stopped because his thumb grazed over her lips. "We're not going to make love because we want a baby," he said. "We're going to make love because we know so many wonderful ways to express our love with our mouths and bodies. It will not be to make a baby. As a matter of fact, tonight I forbid it. Absolutely no baby-making. That's a rule. Don't try to cheat and make one behind my back."

Laura chuckled. She hated to say so—especially since his mentioning the wonderful ways they knew to express their love had nudged desire to life in her—but they could not make love now. "Joe's coming," she told him. "You should be leaving about now to pick him up."

Michael reached for the phone beside the bed, dialed, and, while waiting for his call to be answered, kept stroking Laura seductively. "Hello, Jeannine? This is Michael Daniels. I'm fine, Jeannine. How are you?" A few seconds later he said, "Hi, Joe. Look, I'm going to be late, about an hour late. Is that all right? . . . Good. Okay, I'll see you later."

He hung up.

"We could put the groceries away first," Laura said. "We'd still have plenty of time."

Michael told her the only thing they were going to do with the groceries was put them out of their minds. When they both were undressed, he cupped her face in his hands and said, "Ground rules. First, no baby-making. No thinking about it. No worrying. We're going to extract every ounce of sensual pleasure from each other that is humanly possible to extract. Then, when we've finished doing that, the fun's really going to begin. Think you can take it, Mrs. Daniels?"

Laura laughed. "Mr. Daniels, I'm a giver, not a taker,

remember? And with what I have to give right now—
watch out!"

Thirty minutes later she wondered idly, and without any
emotion resembling worry, if inadvertently they might
have broken rule one.

CHAPTER ELEVEN

It was their great fortune to find a house that suited them, and the two-story natural wood home with gable roofs was already nearing completion. The family that had intended to live in the house had moved east because of a marvelous job offer. Laura and Michael were amazed, as they watched the house being finished, at how closely the other couple's taste matched their own.

The size was not excessive, but there would be an office for Laura, a room and bath for Joe, a second guest room for visitors from California, and a family room, where the railroad layout would be a star attraction. Outside there would be a barn with stalls for their horses.

Laura was especially excited about the kitchen. The sun-filled country kitchen was next to the solarium breakfast nook, the large family room, and the raised dining room. Another special feature was the redwood deck that encircled the house where the summer months, over all too quickly, could be enjoyed to the fullest.

Some of the joys of this home would be luxuries—a fireplace in the master bedroom and a huge master bath with a sunken oval tub. Other attractions would just make life more comfortable for the Danielses. There was a big mud room—something people who lived their lives in Southern California probably never heard of. The little house Laura and Michael lived in now did not have room for a microwave oven, a dishwasher, or a freezer, and Hisega was not near any supermarket. The new home would have all these appliances and a big pantry with built-in spice racks—boons to Laura, considering her full working schedule.

Besides its functional attractions, the new kitchen had decorator accents that danced through Laura's head and practically made her clap her hands in eager anticipation. A luminous ceiling would brighten the spacious room on dark days. There was a center island with a grill. Gleaming decorator tiles with bright vegetables—carrots, tomatoes, peppers, eggplant, and peas—would match the wallpaper.

Laura loved it all. She thought that her new kitchen should be featured in interior design texts as well as in magazines. She was so enthusiastic about cooking she had already bought several cookbooks, including one on bread baking. Life without Luisa and a wide array of accessible restaurants had already changed Laura's domestic habits. Now she was looking forward to delving more deeply into the culinary arts. She had bought a wok and a large clay cooking pot.

"Do you think I could run a restaurant or be a chef?" Laura asked idly when she, Michael, and Joe were on the pontoon at Pactola one Sunday afternoon.

She had finished working on her column and writing personal answers to design questions and was now leafing through the current issue of *Gourmet* magazine.

Michael and Joe were fishing, with Joe having the greater success. When Laura looked up from the magazine to ask the question, she saw, as she often did, how beautifully Michael and Joe complemented each other. Michael had classically good looks. Joe, with a different heritage, would grow up to have a different type of male beauty. Right now he was darling. His illness had not made him frail-looking. On the contrary, he had strong shoulders for his age and a solid, sturdy look.

It was their personalities that were uncannily alike, Laura thought. They could be father and son, as if the months of companionship had caused a subtle blending of personalities. Although Joe was quieter than Michael, he was just as warm and generous. He was creative and had a great respect for nature, as did Michael.

Michael had always been attracted to what the earth offered up; if his father hadn't pressured him to choose a life in business, she knew he would have become a geologist. He had a lifelong fascination with minerals. In South Dakota, she thought, he had extended his love of nature. Here he didn't just live near forests and lakes, but he understood them. He hunted and understood why he was doing it. Laura had learned how to prepare many venison dishes and how to present a succulent pheasant, and Joe prided himself on his deer jerky. He would make it in the Danielses' kitchen, then take most of it home to his cousins in Rapid City. Michael, though, was always in charge of cooking fish.

When Laura asked if she would make a good restaurateur or chef, Michael shook his head thoughtfully before answering, "I'm afraid to tell you it's possible. You might fit it into your schedule."

Laura chuckled, even though she had a quick piercing memory of the only real fight they'd had in South Dakota. *Or are you planning on taking another job?* he had asked. *Is there something to do with decorating that you can fit in between midnight and dawn?* Michael was smiling at her now. He hadn't thought of that bitter accusation when he joked about her schedule; she was sure he hadn't. He was just being playful. "What do you think, Joe?" Laura asked. "Michael won't give me an honest answer."

132

The boy looked sincere as he said, "I love everything you cook. I never ate this good before you came here."

Restraining a parental urge to correct his grammar, she smiled and said, "Thank you, dear."

"You make the table so pretty, too," Joe added.

Laura felt as if she'd been given a bouquet. She felt like hugging Joe. She had received countless compliments on her decorating skills over the years, but none had warmed her as much as Joe's simple words of appreciation.

"I'm warning you, Joe. Compliment her like that, and you're playing right into her hands. She'll open a chic French restaurant in Keystone or Spearfish, and we'll never see her again."

"I could see her," Joe said to Michael. "If Laura has a restaurant, I'll want to go to it a lot. I could even help in the kitchen and clear the tables."

Although mature for his age, Joe was guileless. Laura wondered if he realized that Michael was joking. Then, looking lingeringly at her handsome husband, she wondered if he *was* joking. She sensed that although he was happy with their life at this juncture, he was truly disturbed by how much she was doing. He'd never mentioned it, after the fight, but if he did bring it up, she would have to agree with him. Her career was comprised of supposedly part-time jobs. But part-time jobs, she'd learned, grew like grass in summer.

Her social life was also burgeoning. She thought of it as *her* social life because even though they went to parties as a couple, she knew that Michael didn't need the parties. He had made a few close friends, but they were not in the country club set that Laura seemed to be involved with more and more. Although Michael was always gracious at these affairs, he was bored by them.

They were going to a dinner party at the club tonight.

133

Laura felt so relaxed on the pontoon she would just as soon not go into Rapid City, but a good client was having what she called a small dinner. Well, it would just be a few hours; they could be the first to leave. *Of course we'll go,* she thought. *And it wouldn't hurt Michael to be a little bored for a few hours or Joe to be home alone.* He seldom had the chance to experience solitude. And he didn't mind staying alone, especially now that they had the Labrador pup named Prince. Laura would fix Joe a hamburger, salad, and corn on the cob before she dressed to go out. Joe would spend the time they were away playing with Prince and with his electric train set. Michael had been skeptical about getting the train layout. He'd thought that Joe might lose interest in it after the newness had worn off. But Laura was happy to see that instead Joe was reading everything the Rapid City Public Library had to offer on railroads in America. Tonight, while she and Michael were at the party at the Arrowhead Country Club, Joe would round out the evening by reading a book about trains and eating a head of iceberg lettuce.

Just as this thought was making Laura smile to herself, Michael looked over Joe's head at her and said, "Do we absolutely have to go tonight? Wouldn't you love to stay home? Maybe go over to the new house and ogle it for a while?"

Laura laughed, but she noted that the look on Michael's face was serious. He really didn't want to go, she realized suddenly. The people at the party meant nothing to him. He had all he wanted at home: his wife, his Little Brother, and his well-behaved dog, his plans for the new house and the new Ornery Ore that was going to open in Deadwood in the fall. She wished she could give him the Sunday evening he wanted. But it was too late, of course, to cancel.

"I wish you'd stay home," Joe said.

Laura saw the frown that crossed Michael's face. He kept his gaze on the lake's placid surface, and his features were inscrutable. But the frown had been there, like the shadow of a cloud.

"I thought you liked it when we went out, Joe," Laura said. "Isn't it nice to have the house all to yourself—just you and Prince?" She hoped he would say that he did like it and say it very convincingly.

"Sure. It's nice. It's better than going back to sleep at my aunt's. Especially now."

Laura didn't have a chance to ask him what "especially now" meant. Michael beat her to it, and as he asked the question, she could see that the answer was extremely important to him. She thought that Michael must fear his prediction had come true: that they had spoiled Joe in Hisega and he was no longer satisfied living with his aunt.

"It's nothing."

"I'd rather you finish what you started to tell us, Joe," Michael said quietly but firmly.

Joe looked embarrassed. His face reddened as he admitted that another aunt and her two children had moved into the house. This aunt and her son and daughter loved to eat sweets. The son, Joe's cousin Eddie, kept trying to tempt Joe to eat candy bars. He told Joe that the doctors had lied to him because they hated Indians. He said that Joe really didn't have diabetes and that sugar wouldn't hurt him.

"I told him about the times I had to go to the hospital, but he said I was poisoned so I'd think I had diabetes."

"How old is this Eddie?" Michael asked. Laura could feel the tension in Michael, the restraint of surging anger. It was nearly palpable, as if the pontoon had walls and a ceiling and Michael's strong emotions were filling a small airless space.

Her own emotions were bursting inside her. She wanted

135

to throttle Eddie. How cruel of him to use Joe's illness as a weapon against him. Cruelty was always appalling, but in the young it was unfathomable to her.

"He's twelve. The other kids call him Fat Eddie. He eats candy all day. He hates me, Michael. He really does. I don't know why. He says if I don't do what he says, he'll hide my insulin."

Michael muttered something under his breath, turning his head away from Joe as he did so.

Joe was silent a moment, and then he blurted out, "I can handle it, Michael. Don't worry."

Laura felt a stab of tenderness for both of them. Michael's emotions were fatherly; he wanted to protect Joe from any kind of abuse. Joe's feelings toward Michael were oddly similar. He wanted to protect his older friend—his only real father figure—from having to share the trouble in his life.

"I'm glad you told us, Joe. You shouldn't have to carry a problem like that all by yourself," Laura said. "Would you like me to come to your house and talk to your aunt Jeannine about Eddie?"

"No. I don't want to bother her. She has a lot of problems," he said gravely. "It's okay. I don't listen to Eddie. He wants to fight me, but I won't fight. He says he's going to beat me up anyway, and when I'm unconscious, he'll tell his mother and Aunt Jeannine that I'm in a diabetic coma."

Laura felt sick to her stomach. The thought of poor Joe having to live with a bully who made such outlandish threats was unbearable. She wanted to beg Michael to do something about it. But what could be done?

We could keep Joe here all the time, she thought. *We could adopt him.*

It wasn't the first time Laura had had this thought, but

she had never mentioned it to Michael. Now she wondered if she had avoided talking about adopting Joe because to discuss it would make it become reality. Michael would love to be Joe's father; of that there was no doubt. But was she really capable of being his mother? They came from such different worlds. Joe's grandparents and parents had lived on the reservation. He had never been outside western South Dakota. The relationship between Indian and white man in South Dakota, Laura had learned, was in general not good. Each seemed to disdain and mistrust the other. The kind of family fidelity and generosity that made it impossible for Joe's aunt Jeannine not to take in three more people when her small house was already overcrowded made the majority population shun having Indians for neighbors.

Laura had first learned of this bias against Indians over lunch one day at the Hotel Alex Johnson several months before. The woman had said, "If a nice Indian family of six moves into the house next door to you, you're probably going to have ten more people in that house within a month. An Oglala Sioux can't say no to a relative in need. He would cut out his tongue first. If you hire one, and he seems like a good employee the first week, the next week he doesn't show up for two days. On the third day he comes in at eleven and says his aunt got sick and he's been nursing her. A week later he shows up at eleven again, this time because his cousin needed to borrow his car the night before and didn't bring it back. So he had to walk twenty miles to work. I tell you, you can't deal with these people as neighbors or employees."

Another woman quickly interjected, "You can't compliment a Sioux on a piece of jewelry that you like, or she'll insist on giving it to you."

Laura had listened, feeling bad but intending to keep

137

silent on the subject. Finally, she had to say something. "I don't think I would mind dealing with people whose worst faults were generosity and compassion," she said. "If all the Sioux are like that, they seem like wonderful people."

There had been an awkward pause. Then the topic was changed.

That had taken place several months ago. Now, on this lulling August afternoon, she was on an exquisite lake thinking about how much she loved one Indian boy and hated another. She wanted to adopt Joe. She wished Eddie were on the pontoon so she could push him overboard.

"I think I'll take you and Eddie fishing next week, so the three of us can talk," Michael said to Joe. "We'll educate him a little bit about diabetes and let him know we really think it's not right for anyone to be teased because he's overweight. You know, Joe, that Eddie doesn't have a father to talk things over with now, and he knows that you've got me to talk to. I'm not your father, of course, but we're very close. Eddie knows that. How about our getting him into the Big Brothers program. Do you think he'd go for that?"

Joe nodded enthusiastically at the question, but Laura had seen a prior response to Michael's words. She didn't know if Michael had noticed, but when he said, "I'm not your father, of course," Joe had looked down at his fishing reel and seemed to pull into himself. He'd sucked his lips in so hard they were momentarily hidden from view.

Joe's making sure he doesn't blurt anything out, Laura thought. She, too, was keeping from blurting out the obvious truth. Michael *was* Joe's father. He was this dear child's father because nobody else was and because Joe had placed all his trust in Michael.

It will happen, Joe. I'll see that it does. Just wait awhile, honey, she vowed silently.

Exhilaration flooded her suddenly. But she said nothing out loud. *Joe, you'll soon be our son. We'll always love you,* she thought and resumed reading her magazine, a smile on her face.

She couldn't concentrate on a single line. She wanted to adopt Joe this afternoon, before somebody else got the notion to do it. What if that happened? A lot of enlightened couples—even singles—were adopting older children. She swept her gaze around the undeveloped lakeside, as if expecting someone to get into an evil-looking sleek black motorboat and race out to their pontoon to snatch Joe out of their life.

But as much as she wanted to adopt Joe Kills Deer, she wanted to have her own child. She was beginning to think that she was pregnant, but hadn't hinted this to Michael. She couldn't bear to disappoint him if it wasn't true.

She had an appointment to see an obstetrician the next day, so tomorrow evening she would tell Michael she was pregnant or tell Michael she wanted to adopt Joe, or perhaps she would tell Michael she was pregnant and wanted to adopt Joe.

Maybe she would tell Michael how she felt about Joe tonight, after the party, and tell him about the pregnancy tomorrow night. All this was overpoweringly joyous to contemplate. She was so happy she even forgot she wanted to punch Fat Eddie's lights out.

CHAPTER TWELVE

The party at the Arrowhead Country Club began early in the evening. It was boring for Laura, so she knew it had to be excruciatingly dull for Michael. She was glad that it was still fairly early when they were on their way home.

Michael was too quiet. The set of his face, in profile, was too aloof for someone who had merely been inconvenienced by a little boredom.

Laura studied his unmoving features, wondering what the problem was. Then she turned her attention back to the dark countryside. *I've got to cut down on our social engagements,* she thought. *I've got to cut down on my work hours, too. He's becoming resentful, and I can't blame him.*

She was bringing work home nearly every evening. Her weekends were more than half-filled with work. Between the furniture store, the class, the column, the new house, and trying to participate in at least some outings with Michael and Joe, she was worn-out. She loved all these pursuits, but sometimes she felt like a dog chasing its tail.

Priorities, she muttered to herself. *Priorities, priorities.*

She looked at Michael again. Was he angry about the evening for some reason? "Okay, it was a boring party," she said with a smile.

He didn't answer.

"Oh, honey. I'm sorry. I'll make up for it. Next weekend we won't go *anywhere* except out on the lake."

"Fine."

Oh, boy. He was madder than mad.

"Two weekends," she said with a gentle smile. When he didn't even attempt a return smile, she asked tentatively, "Three? Four? Nothing social until Christmas?"

"Laura, I don't mind socializing."

"I *thought* you minded. You don't seem very happy." After the next two seconds of silence she appended, "With me."

"Maybe I'm not very happy with you."

She turned to face him. "What did I do, Michael?"

"You honestly don't know, do you?"

"Darling, if I knew, I would have already said I was sorry. Or, if I didn't think I was in the wrong, I would feel unjustly accused and I'd be as angry as you are. But no, dear, I *don't* know."

"Forget it. It doesn't matter."

"Michael!" She stared at him openmouthed for a moment, then spluttered, "What on earth *is* it? This isn't like you! And you're doing the same thing you asked Joe not to do this afternoon. When he told us he had a problem at home but then didn't want to follow through with an explanation you didn't like it—remember?"

"I don't think this is a problem that can be rectified," Michael said sternly.

"Try me!"

Laura spoke more forcefully than she wanted to. She wanted to keep very calm, so that whatever accusation Michael leveled at her would be seen in a clear light, not in the blinding light of hysteria. Despite her good intentions, she didn't feel calm.

"It's your attitude about what and who I am, Laura. That attitude is ingrained. It can't be changed."

"My—my *what? My attitude?"*

141

What was he talking about? She adored him, pure and simple. It was admiration of his character, respect for his ideals, and an unrelenting desire to gaze upon his face, her fingers through his hair, and ravage his lithe and muscular body as often as she could. Her attitude toward what and who he was began and ended with love. Right now, though, she felt defensive. She had no idea why he was angry with her and felt he was being very unfair.

"Let's skip it," Michael snapped. He shrugged, shifted his hands on the Blazer's steering wheel, and riveted his eyes to the road.

"Michael, I thought that *my* anger this afternoon, at Joe's cousin Eddie, was impressive anger. But I was wrong. *Now* I'm angry! At you!"

"Well, then, everything is balanced."

"It's meaningless. That's all it is," she snapped. "If we don't talk it out, it's meaningless."

"Then it's meaningless."

And that seemed to be his last word on the subject. She turned away from him. Sadness began to push anger aside. They were taking this unnecessary grief home to Joe, who was probably happily awaiting their arrival. Joe was a sensitive child. He would know that something was wrong and would feel awkward and insecure. He'd have been better off in Rapid City with Fat Eddie making him miserable.

She had planned to tell Michael in bed tonight that she wanted to be Joe's mother. She had wanted to go to sleep on that beautiful note and have the joy of the adoption-to-be with her when she went to the doctor's office tomorrow. Come what might, she and Michael would be parents.

Now she wouldn't tell Michael in bed that she wanted to adopt Joe. She probably wouldn't even say good night to Michael.

This could have been the most beautiful night, she

thought. They would have kissed Joe good night, gone happily to their room, talked eagerly while caressing each other, and then slipped into effortless, soul-satisfying lovemaking.

Phooey.

"Okay, let's talk it out."

Laura nearly jumped to attention. "What did I do wrong?" she asked quickly, as if by waiting one extra second she might give Michael an excuse to change his mind about talking and keep his stony silence.

"Do you remember when you introduced me to the Goodwins, and Kent said, 'I understand you have a rock shop in Keystone'?"

Laura nodded.

"What information did you volunteer to the Goodwins?" Michael asked, eyeing her angrily for a second.

Oh, God. She looked away from Michael as her guilt sank in, and as it did, she sank farther into the Blazer's seat. A lump of misery cascaded to a thudding halt in her stomach. So that was it: her mentioning that Michael used to own a men's clothing business with stores in Beverly Hills, Corona del Mar, and Santa Barbara.

"Don't you remember?" Michael said. "You threw out the vital information with so much enthusiasm I'm surprised you can't recall it."

"I recall it." She sighed. "Execute me."

"It isn't funny. A joke won't erase it. And I don't think I'm being cruel this time."

"No, Michael, maybe you're not." Laura leaned her head against the headrest and turned to face him again. She gazed at his stern profile for a long moment before saying, "Honey, you aren't being cruel, but a sense of humor on your part could erase it. It was a simple mistake and doesn't have to be a black mark against me."

143

"It seems that the black mark is against me, Laura, because I'm just the proprietor of a rock shop. My God, that must be hard for you to swallow in your social life. I mean, you have status. Besides having a good career going, you're an instructor at a college and a newspaper columnist. You're sought out by people who *never* would have imagined themselves entertaining a rock shop owner. Do you suppose your friends think my vocation is a temporary aberration? A mid-life crisis that will pass? Speculation on where I'll open the next trio of Michael Daniels shops must be wild. What's your guess? Hill City, for the lumberjack trade? Deadwood, to pull in the miners?"

"My guess is that you're judging me unfairly, that you're making a mountain out of a molehill, that I exercised a little poor judgment when talking to the Goodwins, and that this evening is now ruined for three people: you, me, and Joe."

"If all that is true, I'm sorry. Please accept my apology," Michael said coldly.

Without looking at him, she said, "Why don't you . . . balance your apology on your head?"

"Was the party nice?" Joe asked when Laura and Michael walked into the cabin. He had a book open on his lap, a bowl with half a head of lettuce left in it at his side on the sofa, and an unnibbled-at leaf of lettuce in his hand.

"Real nice," Michael said, bending to pet Prince.

"How's the book, honey?" Laura asked as she kissed Joe's forehead.

"Pretty good. Somebody called. I took a message. It was a long-distance call."

Laura headed for the kitchen quickly. The rule of the house was that messages were to be written down and left on the kitchen counter. She hoped fervently that her mother wasn't ill.

The message, in Joe's neat, small handwriting, said: "Zale Winters called."

Laura heard Michael call out, "Was it your mother?"

"No," she answered quietly. "It was Zale . . . Zale Winters."

Michael felt awful, as he watched Laura kiss Joe good night and heard her tell him that she was awfully tired and needed to go to bed early. He wanted to follow her to the bedroom, but he didn't. Instead he stayed up with Joe, and within a few minutes he began to feel better. They got into one of their long and easy conversations that would go on until Joe was too sleepy to talk anymore.

Michael loved these talks. He knew that through them he and Joe were growing closer to each other. The bond between them was continually tightening. Joe was not his son or his real little brother. But this was not a temporary relationship; Michael had known that from the beginning. Sometimes, when they talked, he wished fiercely that Joe were his son. Tonight was one of those times.

When Joe finally fell asleep, Michael washed up and went to the bedroom. He saw Laura propped up against pillows covered by yellow daisy and violet print cases. The August nights were a little warm, and having got out of the silk ensemble she'd worn to the party, she now wore only an oyster silk satin teddy. There was a touch of lace between her breasts and more than a touch above her thighs and hips.

With dogged concentration on the book she was reading, she ignored him.

He sat down on the bed. "Good book?" he asked.

"Not bad."

145

"Nothing like a good book."

"Nothing."

"Or a bad husband."

She didn't answer but looked angrier as she continued to read.

Michael slipped the book out of her hands. She didn't resist, but while forfeiting the book, she held fast to her cross expression.

He glanced at a paragraph in the middle of the page she'd been reading, then bent the corner of the page down and closed the book.

"I don't like bent corners. It's wrong to do that to a book," Laura said icily.

He opened the book, unbent the corner, smoothed it till it lay flat, and closed the book. "It'll be fine," he said, keeping himself from chuckling out loud. He placed the book on the bedside table.

"You lost my place!"

"Nope. I didn't. Here's your place." With that he pulled her onto his lap. She resisted somewhat, but he was by far the stronger of the two.

Laura wriggled and tried to get off his lap, but he held her in place, caressing her as he did so. She was so satin smooth all over that he didn't want to stop his hands even if she decided to stay still.

"I don't *feel* like being on your lap just now, Michael!" Laura said forcefully. But she spoke in a low tone so Joe wouldn't hear.

"You'll feel like it in a minute," Michael told her, "as soon as I apologize to you."

"You apologized in the car!" she snarled.

"But I didn't mean it. That was shoddy. There's nothing more hypocritical than an insincere apology. I'm going to try never to do that again."

"Good! Try! Now let me get off your lap."

"Laura, please don't go. I *am* sorry. I've had time to think about being sorry, and now I really am." Michael's hand cupped Laura's firm and well-rounded hip, and he began to make gentle circular strokes with his hand against her hip. His other hand stroked her smooth skin from throat to wrist, lingering at her shoulder and the crook of her elbow. He lifted her hand and placed it against his cheek. "There," he said. "You slapped me, and I richly deserved it." Then he kissed her hand.

While his lips grazed her palm, she muttered coldly, "You've had time to wonder why Zale Winters is calling. That's what you've had time for."

He removed his mouth from her hand slowly, and his fingers lightly encircled her wrist. He studied his fingers and her wrist, thinking that he would like to design a bracelet and have it made for Laura. Sapphires. Yes. Sapphires and diamonds.

"You used to be jealous of Zale, and you still are," she said when he didn't answer her challenge.

"No, I'm not jealous." Michael wrested his gaze from her wrist and looked deep into her turquoise eyes. What perfect gems those were; how they sparkled. "Don't try to make me jealous," he said softly to Laura, while feasting on those eyes. "There are two good reasons why you can't."

"What are they?"

"I'll tell you what they are on one condition. You accept my apology, and we make mad, passionate, quiet love."

"Those are two conditions," Laura said with a sniff.

He could detect a smile trying to assert itself, at least in her eyes, if not on her lips. And he smiled broadly in return. "You're right, love. But there has to be a condition for each of the two reasons why you'll never make me jealous."

"Then don't tell me the reasons, *love*. Because there's no way I'm going to accept both conditions, especially one of them."

"There's no way you're not."

They stared at each other; she blinked first.

"Okay. You'll have your choice of which condition to accept," Michael said. "The reasons are . . ."

He said this with a flourish and paused. If Laura's smile weren't winning over her scowl, the way the glorious sun always wins over one paltry gray cloud, he would eat both his conditions.

"Reason number one is that I'm the guy you gave up the *Los Angeles Times,* exciting restaurants, and seeing the ocean for. The fact that you did that makes me impervious to things that spark jealousy in other men. Oh, maybe you would have given up See's candy if another man had tried to extricate you from the glittery grip of Beverly Hills. But the *Times?* The ocean? The Music Center? Only one man can get a woman to give up all of that. The one she really loves.

"Reason number two is that you are the goddess of all men's fantasies," he told Laura solemnly. "Jealousy on my part would be ridiculous. Jack Kennedy might as well have become jealous of the swarms of men who ogled Jacqueline. Joe DiMaggio might as well have minded the hordes drooling over Marilyn Monroe."

"I think Joe DiMaggio minded," Laura commented.

"I think I love you," Michael murmured. "But from now on do me a favor. Introduce me to people as a former clothier whose clientele numbered the rich and famous. It will be a conversation starter. Everybody buys clothes. Sometimes people hear what I do now and their eyes go

148

vacant. They don't know what to say next. Even 'How's business?' seems a dubious choice, since they doubt if rock shops do any business. So tell them I used to sell ties and suits. I love you so much, Laura. I love you more than all the ties and suits in all the men's stores in the world and more than all the minerals in the earth. Will you please accept my apology, darling?"

Her smile was pure gold. He held on to it with his smiling eyes and cherished it with his happy heart.

"No," she said, shaking her head slowly and moistening the center of her lower lip with her tongue.

"You won't?"

"Of course not. I'm choosing only one of your two conditions, remember? If I accept the apology, I can't accept the other condition, that we make—"

She never finished the sentence. Michael put his mouth gently over hers and kissed her tenderly.

When their lips parted, Michael eased Laura off his lap. He laid her back against the flowered pillows. Without breaking the silence of the moment by the slightest sound he opened the two snaps that held Laura's teddy closed between her thighs.

Michael felt satisfied from head to toe and forgiven. A few of his peaceful words to Laura were "Tonight was our first fight in two months, angel. That's spacing them too close together. I'll try to behave myself, so we won't fight so often."

"Okay, try," she said with a giggle. "You're going to have to behave yourself, to be a good role model for Joe when he's our son."

Michael quickly disengaged himself from her, propped

himself on an elbow, and, grinning from ear to ear, asked, "Mean it?"

"Mean it!"

Michael rolled on top of her and let out a war whoop.

CHAPTER THIRTEEN

Laura managed to restrain Michael. He wanted to go immediately into the other room and tell Joe that he was going to be their son. Laura said that they didn't dare tell him before they spoke to his aunt. They had to find out if there was any reason that Joe couldn't be adopted.

"I'll call her right now," Michael offered eagerly, getting up from the bed. He was naked, as Laura was, and he quickly stepped into a pair of navy blue low-rise briefs.

"Michael! It's nearly midnight! Do you want to scare her half to death?"

He had to concede that the hour was not appropriate for a phone call, especially to a house where two women were probably sleeping off the exhaustion brought on by caring for eight youngsters.

"Really, to be on the safe side and not take any chance of breaking Joe's heart, we shouldn't tell him until we talk to an attorney," Laura said.

She had to chuckle when she saw the look of consternation that shadowed Michael's features. "Oh, honey, *nothing* will go wrong," she added quickly. "Nobody will want to keep us from having him, but since there's a one in a billion chance of something going wrong, let's be cautious. I just couldn't bear to hurt Joe."

Michael sat down on the edge of the bed. He said, "Laura, all of a sudden I'm scared."

Laura sat up and rested her head on his shoulder. She ran her fingers lightly along the top of the waistband that was snug at his lower back. Her hair fell over his tanned chest, and she felt him raise a hand to stroke it. She had known, even before he touched her silken hair, what he was going to do. She knew him so well that she could predict most of his responses to her. But she hadn't expected his joy over adopting Joe to give way to fear. She stroked his spine, then laid her palm flat to soothe his back with circular massaging strokes.

Michael had been afraid only once before as far as she knew; that was when he feared that their opulent life-style in Beverly Hills was eroding their values. He had faced that fear and acted on it—however painfully—so that it had ceased to exist. He had taken enormous risks. Laura knew that he would act courageously again, that any obstacle presenting itself as they tried to adopt Joe would be overcome by Michael's perseverance and courage.

Nothing would keep them from giving Joe their love. What she cherished in Michael, right now, was his willingness to feel and acknowledge fear. He was man enough to admit what he couldn't bear to have happen to him. Laura knew, from past experience, that he was also man enough to alter circumstances so there would be nothing left to fear.

"Whatever the obstacles, we are going to be Joe's parents," Michael said decisively.

"I know, honey."

"We'll see a lawyer tomorrow morning, and we won't leave his office until we know what's what."

"Michael, don't worry. I have faith. I *know* that it will be all right."

"I just have this crazy, nagging fear. It's irrational, of

course, but I'm afraid someone will come out of the wood-work and say we can't have Joe."

"I had that fear, too, on the lake this afternoon. I was watching you and Joe fish and thinking of how much I wanted to be his mother. Then I got all shivery and nervous. I thought someone would motor out to our pontoon and snatch Joe away from us."

"You had decided this afternoon that you wanted to adopt him?"

Laura nodded against his shoulder. She lifted her head and looked dreamily at his intense expression. Smiling, she lifted a hand to smooth the worry from his brow. "I was full of secrets from you today," she said softly and not just a little mischievously.

Michael's features softened as Laura kissed him over and over again. She touched his brows, thinking that some-day these dark, beautiful brows would be silver, and she would still love caressing them. She touched his lips; they were so sensual. She had always thought they were one of Michael's most provocatively masculine parts.

"What other secret were you keeping from me, mystery lady?" Michael murmured.

"I'll tell you, but only if you promise not to worry. Say that you won't stay awake worrying about Joe and that you won't stay awake worrying about what I'm going to tell you now."

"I won't stay awake," Michael dutifully said.

"How can I be sure?" Laura asked, trailing the backs of her fingers over the midnight shadow of his jaw. She loved this part of him, too; women whose men were bearded were deprived of this intimate awareness of how daily, like the moon and stars coming out, maleness reasserted itself.

"The only way I can think of to convince you that I

153

won't stay awake is to fall asleep right now, before you reveal your secret. Do you want me to do that?" he asked.

"Unh-unh." She shook her head, then tossed it back.

Michael caught a fistful of her hair and wrapped it around his hand. "Speak to me, Laura," he said.

"Darling, I think I'm pregnant. I'm going to a doctor tomorrow. Do you think you can stand becoming a father twice in one year?"

"Oh, my angel, I'll try to hold up," Michael said gratefully.

"Now do you think you can sleep tonight?" Laura smiled.

"No."

"You promised."

"Laura, how sure are you that you're pregnant?"

"I'm ninety-nine percent sure. I shouldn't have told you, though. That other one percent could break your heart."

"No, it couldn't do that. I have you, and together we have Joe. Just tell me this: When do you think this ninety-nine percent probable miracle happened?"

Laura lay down on the pillows, laced the fingers of both hands with Michael's fingers, and brought them down to her belly. "The evening we had the big blowup and then made up. After you made me promise there would be no baby-making that night."

"You made one behind my back?"

"I think I did."

"You always did do whatever you wanted, didn't you?"

"Yes. And right now I want to go to sleep."

"Okay. We'll sleep," Michael said reluctantly. He turned the light out and got into bed with Laura so that his chin was resting against Laura's shoulder, and one hand was tucked between her breasts. Just as Laura was drifting off to sleep, she heard him say, "If they say we can't adopt

Joe, would you mind if we kidnapped him and ran away to live on a desert island? I'd have to help you deliver the ninety-nine percent probable baby, but I think I could do that."

"How would we live?" Laura murmured sleepily.

"If there are natives, I'll sell rocks to them. You'll decorate their huts."

"Do you know, Michael, I always used to think that whenever you opened your mouth to speak, you said something wise and intelligent?" Laura giggled.

"You don't think my idea of running away with Joe is wise and intelligent?"

"Michael, hush. Go to sleep."

"I love you, Laura. Thank you for the baby and for Joe. Thank you for being mine."

"Keep your promise, Michael," she answered gently. "Go to sleep!"

Joe's aunt said she was very happy about their wanting to adopt Joe. The attorney said that no one would come out of the woodwork to prevent the adoption. He said adopting Joe would be a snap. He also said, "Speaking frankly, not many people want to adopt eleven-year-old diabetic kids who are racially different from themselves. I think you're very special people."

"Joe's special. We're just lucky," Michael said.

Later they went together to the doctor's office, where they learned Laura was indeed pregnant. After that, a little dazed and giggly, they began the drive home to Hisega.

"I should be working today," Michael said, "but it's hard to imagine getting my mind on anything except our kids."

"Me, too," Laura said.

"What about your work, Laura?" Michael asked, and

the lightheartedness of their mood disappeared with his thoughtful words. "Don't you think you do too much? You shouldn't exhaust yourself."

Laura compressed her lips as she thought about it. She agreed with Michael entirely. But what could she give up? When she thought of her various career activities, she looked at them as if they were dear friends. To give up any one of them would be to say good-bye to something special in her life.

"I think you enjoy writing the column the most," Michael said.

"Oh, I do, even though so many hours of work go with it."

"Teaching?" Michael asked. "Could you do without that?"

"Mmm, I like it. I like it very much."

"The store?"

"Oh, it's a pain sometimes. But when I have a lot going on there, that is the most invigorating part of my work."

Michael sighed. "You should have been identical twins, and I should be married to you both. One would be a career woman, living in town. Joe and I would never miss her because we'd have the other in Hisega, taking care of us and our baby."

"Polygamy is illegal," Laura said thoughtfully. She was seriously concerned with the problem of having too much work.

"And neglecting your health is a crime," Michael said. "Honey, you don't have time to exercise, and you eat on the run a lot of the time. I want you to have rewarding work, outside our home, but I want you to be healthy, rested, and very sexy. You can't be if you don't find a balance between work and play."

"Michael, can we afford for me not to earn very much

money?" Laura asked. She could see that the question surprised him. It surprised her, too, because she had never given their finances much thought. She'd never asked Michael what their profit from the sale of Michael Daniels had been. She assumed that it had been huge. Now, though, she wanted to know.

His face was rigid as he watched the road in front of them. Once again Laura wondered if Michael missed his former business. Michael Daniels had been more than a trio of successful men's stores; it had symbolized taste and style in three communities where such things mattered a great deal. Why, she wondered, did his face tighten a little whenever she mentioned Michael Daniels? It was as if he were concealing some emotion from her. But her point, in asking about their profit, was that she might give up her work at the store if they did not need her income. Her work for both the newspaper and the college really did not bring in any appreciable funds. "Well," she asked, "did we make a killing in selling the business?"

"Laura, let's not talk money now. Today is too special for that. We should be talking about a first name for Joe's baby brother or sister."

He could not have piqued her curiosity more. She wanted to know what they had made in selling the business. Had something gone awry? Successful businesses often lost their appeal for no apparent reason and became unsuccessful almost overnight. Nowhere could that happen with more dizzying speed than in the quicksilver fashion climate of Southern California. Maybe they had lost a lot of money and were not very well-off anymore. Maybe she should give up the column and teaching and keep the job that brought in a fair amount of money.

"I want to know, Michael, even if the answer is upsetting. Did we take a terrible loss? Please tell me. I've been thinking, just in the last few minutes, that if we could get by without my income as a decorator, I'd like to quit working at the store. Then, except for my course at the college, I could do all my work at home. But if we need the money, Michael, of course I'll continue to work full time."

"We don't need the money. I'll be thrilled if you give up decorating."

He grinned at her, and she could see that he was telling the truth. But she sensed he was hiding something from her. It wasn't like him. She wouldn't ask again, though. When he wanted to tell her, he would.

All right, if he wanted to talk baby names, that was what they would talk about. "How about James Lester, for your father and mine, if it's a boy?" she suggested. "I put your dad's name first because Lester's not that terrific a name. My father never liked it much. And if the baby's a girl—"

"I didn't sell the business." Michael interrupted her quietly in a succession of words that stunned Laura. She sat with her face turned to him, her lips parted in astonishment.

"I still own Michael Daniels, Laura."

"Michael, why didn't I know that? Why did you let me think you'd sold it?" she asked. She was completely confused, at a loss for words. From somewhere deep within she felt betrayed. At the same time she felt a small surge of joy, knowing the stores still belonged to them.

"Did I ever tell you that I had sold it?" he asked.

She didn't answer. No, he never had said that, but he'd certainly led her to believe that he'd made a clean break from his past. *Why?* she asked herself now. *Why did I just assume he'd sold the stores? Because I had to make a clean break,* she answered herself. *I had to give up my hard-won place in the business world, so I took it for granted that Michael had made the same sacrifice.*

"Are you angry, Laura?"

"I—I don't know! Honestly, I don't! I have to think about it."

"At least I get a reprieve." He grinned at her, then said, "What was the girl's name you were going to tell me? I like your choice for a boy."

Laura couldn't remember. She was still too numbed by what he'd revealed to her to think.

They told Joe, in his aunt's home the following afternoon, that they were going to be his mother and father. He looked shy, embarrassed, and very happy all at one time.

Laura looked at Jeannine Kills Deer and saw that she, too, had tears in her eyes. For some reason, the fact that they both were teary-eyed made Laura giggle, and then Jeannine started giggling. Michael laughed out loud. So did Joe. In the span of a moment filled with laughter, the tension inherent in the situation evaporated.

"Would you like to move in with us this coming weekend, Joe?" Laura asked. "I know that you have a lot of friends in the neighborhood to say good-bye to. Would Friday be too soon?"

"I'll just go put my things in a bag and come with you now," Joe said. "Then you won't have to come here and get me on Friday."

Laura smiled. He was trying so hard not to look overly eager and to sound as if he were simply trying to make things convenient for them. "Well," she said, "if it's all right with your aunt, we would like you to come home with us now. That way we won't miss you between now and Friday, and Prince won't have to be lonely for you either."

Before Laura had finished the sentence, Joe looked anxiously at his aunt. Jeannine had shooed the other children outside when the Danielses arrived, so they could talk in a quiet environment. Now the room was hushed as they all awaited what Jeannine would say. Laura knew that the woman was truly happy for Joe and that she would be better off with one less child to care for. Nevertheless, she had been caring for Joe for a long time as if he were one of her own. Laura suddenly felt a stab of sympathy for her. Their gain—hers and Michael's—was this woman's loss.

Jeannine said, "You go get your things."

Joe bolted from the room.

Laura got up from the faded sofa and crossed the small room to where Jeannine sat stiffly on a folding chair. She took the woman's hands in both of hers and leaned down to kiss her cheek. "Thank you," she said.

Jeannine stood up. Laughing a little in her shyness, she said, "I will think of him often."

"We will bring him to see you," Michael assured her. "You'll always be his aunt and a big part of his life. Joe won't forget who gave him a home when he needed one, Jeannine."

Because Joe had so few possessions that weren't already in Hisega, he was back with them in another minute. His aunt rumpled his hair and told him to be good and to be careful to give himself his insulin on time. Then she kissed him good-bye.

"Boy, will Eddie be surprised!" Joe said when they were in the car. "He told me last night that I wouldn't be going to Hisega much longer."

"Why would he say such a thing?" Laura asked, turning to look at Joe in the Blazer's backseat.

"He said that you would have your own son soon, and then you wouldn't want me around. But he was wrong."

Laura stole a quick look at Michael. They had already agreed not to tell Joe about the baby yet. They would let him have "only child" status for a few days. She could see that Michael was mulling over how to deal with this. Poor Michael.

"We *will* have another child, eventually," Michael finally said. "But that child won't be our own any more than you are, Joe. You're not only our own, but our first. The first child is very special to parents. When a baby comes, we'll love it just as much as we love you, even though we had you first. And, Joe, you *are* our own already, even though we haven't got a legal adoption decree yet. You're ours, and we're yours. Agreed?"

Laura smiled, feeling great pride in Michael. He was such a wonderful father. She put her hand on her belly and thought, *As far as fathers go, you're getting the best in the world. You're getting a wonderful big brother and a pretty neat mom, too. You lucky kid!*

When they were nearly home, Michael said, "Joe, right now—while we're still in the car—I'm Michael and this great cook sitting next to me is Laura. But the minute we're inside the house—the very second we walk through the front door—how about starting to call us Mom and Dad? It'll seem strange to you at first, but you'll get used to it soon. Whenever you say Mom or Dad, it will make us very happy. And believe me, we don't need a piece of paper signed by a judge to let us know that we're your folks. We know it already. If you call us Mom and Dad, we'll know that you know it, too. What do you think?"

There was no answer, except for a muffled cry after a few seconds of silence.

Laura turned and reached around to touch Joe's knee. She couldn't get any closer to him just then, because he was strapped to the backseat of the car and she was belted to the front seat. But she could touch him that much and tell him that it was all right to cry.

"The minute we get inside the house, Joe. Okay?" Michael said again as he pulled the Blazer to a stop in front of the cabin that would be their home for two more weeks.

Joe nodded but still didn't say anything. They got out of the car. Prince was inside, and they heard his welcoming bark. Joe carried his grocery bag filled with clothes up the steps. When they were inside, with Prince wriggling around one and then the other's legs, Joe said, "I'll see if Prince's bowl needs water, Mom."

"Thanks, dear," Laura said. Then, after Joe and Prince had scampered from the room, she hugged Michael fiercely.

CHAPTER FOURTEEN

They let Joe have his "only child" status for the rest of the week. Then, on Sunday morning, they told him about the baby. Joe said that he was happy and that he'd always wanted a little brother or sister, but Laura was skeptical. He seemed subdued. When he left the house, saying he was going for a walk, she told Michael that she was worried. "I think he feels threatened," she said. "Oh, how I wish the legal part of this adoption could be over with, so Joe would know that nothing can keep him from really being our son."

Michael didn't act very concerned. He said that all children feel a little subdued when a new baby is on the way. "Any major change makes a kid quiet down and think things over." His calm tone, Laura knew, reflected a genuine belief that Joe was untroubled about the baby. He added, "Joe's going through several major changes at one time. Getting us. The new house. A new school and friends. And now the baby. He can handle it, though. He'll perk up when we pick raspberries this afternoon, especially since he can look forward to having a piece of raspberry pie tonight."

Laura sighed and smiled to herself. Joe did not get to eat sweets often, and when he did, the evidence of his enjoyment was ample.

Laura and Michael had become knowledgeable about

163

Joe's illness. They had had a consultation with his doctor and had attended a class at the local hospital on controlling childhood diabetes. They'd also bought several books on the subject. Knowledge eased some of the worry for Laura. She had a solemn respect for the seriousness of diabetes but was optimistic about Joe's future.

She no longer winced inwardly when she watched him give himself his daily shot. She no longer resented the fate that made a child take time out from his daily activities to give himself an injection of insulin and check his urine for sugar content. Instead of feeling resentment, she felt grateful that Joe had been born at a time when the diabetic child could grow up to be strong and relatively healthy and when medical science was making advances in controlling the disease.

She felt an extra tug of tenderness for him when he expressed gratitude for her cooking. Today they were going to denude a few stands of wild raspberries that grew near their home, and tonight Joe would get to eat a piece of pie for dessert. He would eat it very slowly, savoring each bite. Laura had never seen a child appreciate special treats the way Joe did. On the rare occasions when he got to eat ice cream, his eyes positively lit up with pleasure.

Joe's eyes had not glowed with pleasure when he'd learned that Laura and Michael were expecting a baby, Laura remembered. She believed him when he said that he'd always wanted a little brother or sister. But she also believed he didn't want a baby brother or sister *now*. He had spent so long surrounded by all those cousins that he must want a period of being the center of attention of his newfound parents, she thought. Despite what Michael had told him about his being their first child, she sensed that he felt very threatened. She hoped he would come back from the walk soon, so she could talk with him and comfort him.

Michael left to go to The Ornery Ore. He would be back at three, and then they would pick raspberries.

Joe didn't return. Laura grew more worried about him as the minutes ticked by. She spent the hours answering letters asking for decorating advice, and also wrote to friends in Beverly Hills. Then she talked on the phone for a while to her mother. Her mother was overjoyed that Laura was pregnant, and the many minutes of their conversation sped by.

Soon after Laura had said good-bye to her mother and hung up, Joe came back. Laura didn't know why, but she felt immense relief. She also felt that she should scold him for staying out so long. He knew how important it was that he have his meals on time. But under the special circumstances of the day she let his tardiness go unmentioned and told him to wash up for lunch. Michael came home and had a snack with Joe, and then, carrying plastic pails, they all trudged off to the raspberry groves.

The bushes were full with ripe red berries just begging to be plucked, and Laura took to the satisfying task with greedy relish. She remembered being at the shore when she was about Joe's age. One morning, very early, she'd gone down to the water by herself. No one else had been on the beach. She'd found the wet sand littered with seashells. Most were broken, but they all seemed wonderful and *very* valuable. She'd felt as if she were a princess as she gathered the treasure trove of broken shells. That was how she felt today, picking the berries. But it was work. She knew she had to be careful not to crush them, and she had all she could do to resist popping them right into her mouth as they came off the bush.

Michael had told her several times he didn't want her to

work too long, and she promised she wouldn't. After a couple of hours she wasn't tired at all and was surprised when Joe announced that he was tired and wanted to go back to the house. She wished he wouldn't and tried to coax him into staying. But he left.

"He isn't happy," Laura said to Michael.

"Honey, nobody is happy every minute of the day every day of the week," Michael answered gently.

Laura couldn't argue with that. They picked berries, quitting only when they felt they had enough for two pies. Then they walked to a nearby grassy slope where they could rest.

"How is James Lester or Leslie Ann feeling?" Michael asked. He began taking off his shirt. It was the pewter knit that he'd worn the afternoon of the big fight. Laura never saw the shirt without remembering the rage and grief of the fight, the healing of reconciliation, and, most of all, the deepened understanding they'd gained of each other's feelings.

"Are you overheated?" she asked, looking fondly at his beautiful bare chest.

"No." He held the shirt up and folded it. Then he placed it on the grass, behind Laura. "There," he said, patting it smooth. "You have a pillow. Lie down. I'll shield you from the sun."

She was all too happy to accept the offer. When she had wriggled her shoulders and hips to get comfortable and received kisses on her forehead, nose, and chin, she said that the baby was fine; it didn't have a care in the world. Then she thought that she wished Joe didn't have a care in the world either.

"We've talked so much about the adoption in the last few days, and the baby, and the new house, and my new shop that we haven't talked about my still being the owner

166

of Michael Daniels," Michael said. "You never did tell me if you were angry or not. Want to tell me now?"

Michael stroked Laura's arm with a blade of grass as he asked the question. The light, feathery touch made her arm feel tingly and cool. "Clever of you, to ask me that after you've given me the shirt off your back," she said accusingly. But what he'd said was true. They had talked of everything that concerned them except that one important issue. During the past few days they had also enrolled Joe in his new school, chosen a name for the baby if it was a girl, lined the kitchen drawers and cabinets in the new house, and gone to a Big Brothers picnic at Sioux Park. Laura realized that they'd both avoided the topic of the business because this week was special, so filled with happiness; they didn't want to risk bringing up a topic that could ruin it.

"Well?"

"The most honest answer I can give you, Michael, is that sometimes I am angry and sometimes I'm not. Mostly I'm not. I know you didn't actually lie to me, but you didn't make a valiant effort to let me know the truth either. That's what makes me angry. Why didn't you?"

"Because I thought that it would be easier for you to make the break from Beverly Hills if you didn't think Michael Daniels still had a claim on my life. If I had talked to you about my keeping the business, you might have thought that making a new life here was a hobby for me—something that could be discarded if I got bored with it."

Laura thought about what he'd said. Then she said, "I can see your point, but I still think you were being manipulative."

"Hell, yes, I was! I wanted you here with me, Laura. I would have gone to any means I could think of to manipulate you."

167

"Okay. I suppose I can understand that, especially since you didn't tell me any outright lies. But I don't understand why you kept the business. Were you afraid that you might get tired of living here and want to go back?"

"No. Never. Not for a moment. I thought that if you didn't come to me—and it seemed for a long time that you wouldn't—I should keep the business so your future would be financially secure. Even if our separation had ended in divorce, Laura, I needed to know that you would never want for anything. The decorating business is more precarious than most. I couldn't have lived with myself if I hadn't provided for your future, and a rock shop—even one of The Ornery Ore's caliber—is not a guaranteed source of income."

"Then why didn't you sell Michael Daniels when I did come here? Our cost of living is minuscule compared to what it was in Beverly Hills. You could have sold the business after I finally made the break."

He sat up, clasped his arms around his knees and gazed at the pure Dakota sky. Laura shielded her eyes with an arm and with her other hand caressed the taut bare skin just above Michael's hips. The skin she touched was as suntanned and smooth as the sky was blue and clear.

Michael looked intently at her as he spoke. "When you came to me, I swore to myself that if you weren't happy here, I would take you back. And I wouldn't resent having to live in Beverly Hills. At least we both would have tried to make a new life. To fail after trying is not the same kind of failure as never having tried. But you—you wonderful woman and wife—made a go of it here. I did start to think of selling the business, of making the final break for both of us. But I also started craving children. I fantasized adopting Joe but never would have told you my fantasy. It had to come from you, or it wasn't going to happen. And I also longed for us to have a baby."

"It just goes to show that the slightest fantasies can come true," Laura said softly.

"Yes. But besides fantasies, there is reality. I started thinking about what I would owe to my kids if I had any. Wouldn't I owe them the advantages only money can buy? Good summer camps, enlightening travel, fine colleges? Rock shops really do not generate wealth. I knew I could invest the money we realized on the business and the sale of our house, but keeping the business seemed to be the wisest investment of all."

Laura sat up. "Michael, why would the kids want to go to expensive summer camps?" she asked. "What would they find there that they can't have right here in the Black Hills? Are any lakes anywhere lovelier than the ones we have all around us? Could our children find better riding or hiking trails than we have right here? Aside from what they'll have in summer, we're twenty minutes from ski slopes in winter. In fall we've got the best thing next to New England, in Spearfish Canyon. Travel? Joe's never been to Paris or Rome, but do you imagine that there is a boy anywhere who is more enlightened by what he's seen of the world than Joe is?"

Michael shook his head and grinned at her simple philosophy. "Laura, my heart, you are one hundred percent wonderful in all ways," he said.

"No, I'm not." She sighed. "I've got something to confess, Michael." She told him the inner reaction she'd felt when she learned they still owned the three men's stores. She said she recognized it as a deep-seated desire to have her cake and eat it, too. She loved her new life, but owning a lucrative business in California kept the old life, which she'd also loved, safely tucked away for possible future use.

169

Even with the events of recent days, she'd thought about it often. And anger that Michael had kept part of their life a secret from her wasn't what came to the fore when she thought about it. Bewilderment about her own attitude was what did.

"It's your business, not mine, but I want you to know that I think it's a crutch. At least it is for me. And as long as I have the option of waltzing back into our old life, I'll never feel fully settled here. We might live here till we're old, but somehow, having the stores in California will always make me feel that this is temporary. Do you see what I mean, Michael?"

"Yep. I do," he answered thoughtfully.

"Sell the stores, honey. Will you?" Even as she said it, she didn't know if she meant it. But she hoped he would say yes.

"Mm, probably. But not right away. I want you to have more time to think about it."

"Do you think I need more time? Don't you have faith in me?" she asked. Her faith in herself had been a little shaken by her unexpected clinging to the past. She thought she'd feel better about herself if she could encourage Michael to make a clean break and if she meant it. There would be no martyrdom involved, just an honest acceptance of their life here.

"Laura, I have so much faith in you it's almost sinful. But I'm going to wait until the baby's born and then ask if you still feel the same. Honey, I want to give you every happiness. I don't want you or our children to be deprived of anything. We could even have two homes—one here and one in Beverly Hills. Living in two places works for lots of families. It's an option. There's no reason we can't do that. We can afford to do it, so why shouldn't we?"

She drew away from him. Looking at him as if he'd just

uttered the most incredible nonsense, she answered, "Why shouldn't we? For openers, neither of us wants to. We've decided to make our lives here. That should be enough reason for both of us."

He was grinning, even as he tried to guide her into accepting his offer. "What about all those things you miss?" he asked. "The *Los Angeles Times* and the ocean? I miss things, too. I miss our rose garden. That was my favorite part of our home."

"I *loved* the rose garden," Laura said. "I loved a lot of things in California, and I miss my mother. But one or two visits out there a year should do me just fine." Laura sealed her statement with a kiss, and just as their lips parted, they heard Joe approaching.

He was out of breath from running to them. His face was red and sweaty. He told them, in hasty sentences, that he was invited to spend the night at his aunt's house. Jeannine had taken her children to Sheridan Lake and had called Joe from the marina there. If Joe could spend the night, she would pick him up on her way back to town.

"Do you really want to?" Laura asked. The conversation with Michael had made her forget her concern about Joe's reaction to the news of the baby. Now she was concerned again. She didn't want Joe to be away for the night. She had planned an evening that just included the three of them.

"Yeah, I want to go," Joe said.

Laura sighed. She told Joe to take one of the pails filled with raspberries and give it to his aunt.

"Don't forget your insulin," Michael said. He told Joe that he was going to Rapid City in the morning and would call to tell him what time he would pick him up.

"Give me a kiss, honey," Laura said.

171

Joe pecked her on the cheek and then ran off with Prince at his heels.

"I wish he weren't going," Laura said.

"Not me."

Laura looked at Michael. "Did I detect a seductive note in your voice?" she asked. He assured her that she had. They lay back down, turned on their sides, and kissed tenderly. "I love it out here," Laura said. "I'll miss picking the berries, until next summer." They were quiet for a few moments. Then she said, "Michael, when you said you missed the rose garden, do you know what that made me think of? I always had a secret desire to make love in our garden, under the stars."

"Why didn't you tell me?" he murmured, gliding his hand over her hip and side, and then bringing it to rest over her breast. "I would have given you your desire."

Laura chuckled. She knew he would have; that was probably why she'd never told him. Although their backyard in Beverly Hills had been fenced and reasonably private, theirs had been a street of two-story houses. It wasn't impossible that someone would have seen Laura's secret desire fulfilled. She had not been uninhibited enough to turn the lovely fantasy into reality.

"We'll do it tonight," Michael murmured. The pressure of his fingers plucking at her nipple through the thin material of her blouse emphasized his eagerness for night's arrival.

"How? We don't have a rose garden now."

"But we have a wild raspberry garden. It's bigger, better, and much more secluded. The stars above it are even brighter. And . . ." He paused and drew a lazy circle around her erect nipple. His knee moved against her leg, then parted her thighs. "And," he continued, "Joe won't be home. There's no better time than tonight for making

172

love beneath the stars. If you prefer roses to raspberries, I'll make you think of roses, my love."

"Don't wait. Make me think of them now."

"Laura?"

She heard the slightly shocked tone in his voice, and she laughed lightly at her own brazen proposal.

The August afternoon was still bright and clear. The sun was still high in the sky. The spot where they rested, while secluded, was not really private. Anyone had the right to come here. Anyone might. Hikers, strollers, berry pickers, dog walkers, bird watchers, or lost children might happen upon their unfenced seclusion. Someone they knew—a neighbor—could happen by. This was even riskier than making love at Mount Rushmore on a winter afternoon, Laura realized. And she hadn't taken that lesser risk.

Yet wasn't that the scent of roses in the air? Weren't those stars above and around her?

Yes, when she closed her eyes and opened her mouth to receive Michael's kiss, there were stars. He had rolled on top of her and then sat up, his legs on either side of hers. His hand opened one button of her cotton blouse, then another—and then another. He slipped the buttons through the openings slowly, expertly.

Laura's silver blue bra hooked in front. Michael's fingers, smelling faintly of raspberries, unhooked it.

Next, he unbuttoned the jeans at her waist. His fingertips trailed idly from her waist to the rim of her silver blue bikini panties, and then the backs of his fingers were against her skin as he slipped them beneath the satiny fabric.

"Don't open your eyes," he murmured.

Laura didn't answer except to smile. Ah, let the bird watchers and berry pickers stroll by and see them; she didn't even care. She wouldn't open her eyes. She would be oblivious to the world. Besides, she wasn't part of the world anymore. Sensually she was adrift in the night sky; each thrill that caused her body to shiver and surge was a gently warm and winking star.

"Don't, angel. Don't open your eyes."

She didn't. She sensed his reaching away from her for a moment. Then he was stroking the curve of her cheek with the tip of his finger.

"Do you feel a rose on your cheek?" he whispered.

She nodded.

He gently stroked her belly. Laura envisioned, behind closed eyes, his fingers holding the long and deep-toned stem of the rose. He was being careful not to touch her with a thorn, not even with a leaf. The kiss of the tight bud made a tour of the outer plumpness of a breast now and then touched the breast's nipple so softly Laura had to clutch at it with her yearning imagination.

Then she didn't feel the rose anymore. Michael gathered her breasts in his hands, leaned his face down to hers, and then grazed his lips over and beneath her chin and down to the hollow beneath her throat. He uncovered her other breast, moistened its tip with his tongue, then blew it dry.

The warm air from his mouth, Laura knew, was a midnight breeze. He pressed his fingers between her thighs, then slid his hand up under her hips, raising her still-clad body for its share of midnight kisses. She arched upward to his mouth and clutched hard at his head as if she were hanging for dear life onto the moon. All the while she kept her eyes tightly closed. She saw brightness within the framework of darkness, for where there were stars and a moon there was light. She could swear that she saw the moon behind her lids and even smelled its mysterious valleys. But most of all, she smelled roses in all stages of their bloom. She felt their beads of dew upon her skin.

They made love tenderly, gently, and with infinite care for what seemed like an eternity. Then slowly, reluctantly, when the late-afternoon shadows were lengthening, they put their clothes back on and left for home.

They made the drive back in silence, not needing words to convey their feelings to each other. But when they walked back into the house, their little dreamworld was immediately shattered.

Laura quickly saw that Joe hadn't taken his insulin with him. She went to the dining room, which served as his bedroom, and saw that he hadn't taken anything with him at all. "Michael!" she called, feeling a sudden sense of panic.

CHAPTER FIFTEEN

"Hello, Jeannine? Hi, this is Michael. Joe forgot to take his insulin to your house, so I'm going to have to drive into Rapid City. Is he around? I'd like to talk to him if he's not outside."

As she listened to Michael's words, Laura was certain that on the other end of the line Jeannine would be looking puzzled—because Joe wasn't there. She practically held her breath, hoping that she was wrong and Michael would, in another second, be talking to Joe on the phone. But the look that came over Michael's face informed her that she'd been right. Joe was not at his aunt's home. He had run away.

"That darned kid," Michael said as he hung up the phone. "When Jeannine came to pick him up, he told her he'd changed his mind and didn't want to go. Wait here, Laura. I'll run out and see if he took his horse."

Laura did as Michael had asked; she didn't move from where she'd been standing in the kitchen except to lean against a counter. When Michael came back inside, a little out of breath from running, and muttered, "His horse isn't gone; he took off on foot," she didn't know whether to be disappointed or relieved.

"Where would he have gone, Michael?" she asked quietly.

He shook his head, shoved his hands into his back pockets, and sighed. Laura knew that he didn't have any more of an idea of where Joe would have gone than she did. "Oh, Michael . . ." She put her palms on Michael's chest. Being as apprehensive as she was, she needed to draw strength from him. But when she touched Michael, she remembered that no sooner had Joe run off from them than they had turned the afternoon into a sensual romantic fantasy. She had forgotten her concern over Joe's insecurity in a moment so that she could revel with Michael in the security of their endless love.

Michael took his hands from his pockets, placed them over hers, and said, "Don't worry. Joe will be back before it's dark. If he's upset about our having a baby, he's just gone off to think about it and work the newness out of his system. He won't stay out all night. He's too conscientious a kid to do that."

Laura thought otherwise, and the fact that he hadn't taken his insulin terrified her.

"He could wind up in the hospital," she said softly. "Michael, we have to look for him. We just can't stay here and wait for him to come back. He *might* be praying that we'll look for him. Please let's go! Let's do something!"

Michael nodded. "Yep" was his succinct response. Afterward, though, he added, "When we do find him, I'm going to tell him my opinion of this kind of attention-getting behavior."

"I'm going to tell him that we love him," Laura said.

"Well, that, too." Michael gathered Laura to him for a hug. "I guess this is what it's like being parents, Laura, and we're nervous about it. Do you think we're making a mountain out of a molehill? Maybe we should sit tight. He *is* making a dramatic bid for attention."

"Michael! Honey! He's making a dramatic bid for our attention because he needs it. We *can't* fail him. We have to show him today that whatever he needs from us tomorrow, he'll get. We have to give him the attention he's asking for, even if it is going to include a stern lecture."

"Oh, is it!" Michael said. "Come on. We'll take the Blazer. He could be walking toward Johnson Siding or toward Trout Haven. Or he could have gone—"

Michael stopped. Laura felt sick to her stomach. He had stopped speculating verbally on where Joe could have gone to because he could have gone to so many places. There were numerous small towns he could have headed for. There were also hills and forests galore to lose yourself in.

"We have to call the sheriff's office," Laura said.

Michael turned and put his hand on the phone. Then he ran his other hand through his hair in frustration. "It's too premature," he said. "For all we know, he's at one of the neighbor's or kicking a stone by the creek less than a quarter of a mile from here."

"He isn't," Laura said. "I feel certain that he isn't."

Michael took his hand from the phone, turned to Laura, and placed his hands against the sides of her head. "Honey, I don't want to call for help yet," he said. "I want to find him myself."

"You don't know which way he went," Laura reminded him. "I keep thinking of more and more places he could have run to. The list seems endless. He could have gone to The Ornery Ore—he loves the shop! He could—"

"I don't think he went to the shop, but I'll go everywhere that it's possible for him to be. I'll leave word, wherever I look, that if anyone sees him, you'll be here to take a call. I'll check in with you when I can get to a phone. Okay, Laura? Will you stay by the phone while I'm searching? Joe might even be the one to call. I wouldn't want him to call and have no one here to answer."

"I'll wait. But it won't be easy."

Michael ducked his face down, to be able to kiss her without making her reach up to him. Then he said, "Who told us being parents was going to be easy? Joe never made that promise," he said, already heading for the door.

Laura followed him. "Michael, don't scold Joe when you find him. You can scold him later."

"Don't worry."

"And tell him that running off when you feel bad is normal. I don't want him to think he did something awful. Tell him—"

"Laura, I can't tell him *anything* if you don't let me go look for him. Now go sit down, and put your feet up."

"I can't," she admitted. "I'm too wound up."

"Then bake us a pie!" he called as he got into the car.

She had thought it a ridiculous suggestion, but after pacing around the house nervously for a while, Laura decided that she actually would bake a pie. At least it would help take her mind off what was happening. She would start by getting the dough ready, and with luck, by the time she was rolling it out on the board, Joe would be home—tired, sheepish, hungry, and contrite. Oh, how she hoped that would happen!

It didn't. She had the pie dough chilling in the refrigerator and had washed the berries, and the oven was preheating. But if she made the pie and put it in the oven, she couldn't leave the house.

I'm not supposed to leave the house, she reminded herself, looking at the telephone for an additional reminder. She had a strong urge to go out on foot and look for Joe. Perhaps Michael had been right when he speculated that Joe could be nearby. The urge to search began to consume her like an itch. But if she left the house, no one would

179

answer if Joe, or Michael, or—heaven forbid—someone from the hospital called.

The thing to do was to bake the pie. If the pie were in the oven, she would effectively be rendered a prisoner here, at least until the oven timer went off.

Laura assembled the ingredients on the counter. Then she stared at them. Bake a pie? How could she? The way worry was weighing on her, she didn't even feel like being near food.

I should do it for Joe, the way he once baked a cake for Michael, she thought. She knew that Joe had bought a packaged chocolate cake mix and canned frosting and had prepared Michael's birthday cake while knowing that he wasn't going to have any himself. The thought made Laura want to do this for him. She began to scan the recipe, thinking that she'd better read it over twice because in her nervousness she was likely to do something wrong.

The phone rang. Laura nearly jumped. *Be Joe,* she prayed, reaching for the receiver.

It was a great disappointment to hear Zale Winters's voice. It was also an invitation to guilt. Laura suddenly remembered that he had called a week ago. She would have called him back, but so much had happened in the past week that Zale's call had been completely forgotten. There was no excuse. It had been unpardonably rude of her, and to top it off, she now had to rush him right off the phone. Quickly she explained that Joe had run away from home and she had to keep the line open in case he called or someone else called to say where he was.

"I won't keep you, Laura," Zale said, sounding concerned. "I'm shocked, though. I didn't realize the boy lived with you."

"We're adopting him!" Laura cried.

"Why, that's wonderful. Congratulations."

Laura realized that what she'd said must have sounded very odd to Zale. She had told him that she and Michael were adopting a child, and the child had run away from home already. Somehow that needed further explanation. "It is wonderful for all of us!" she said. "Joe's very happy about the adoption, but he was upset today because we told him we're going to have a baby."

The author sounded even more surprised, but he congratulated Laura again.

"We'll get in touch with you soon, Zale," she said. "Maybe I'll be able to call you tomorrow."

"No hurry. I really wanted to talk to Michael about a book I'm going to write. It'll be about successful men who walked away from the rat race. But I won't bend your ear about it now. Take care, Laura. Good luck. I'm sure the boy will be home very soon."

After she had hung up, she realized that telling Zale the situation had somehow made her feel even more restless. She could not bake the pie now. She couldn't even stay inside the house. It wasn't big enough to pace her anxiety away in. *And we were making love! Playing a fantasy game about being in a stupid rose garden, while Joe was feeling crushed and miserable!*

That thought constantly came back to her. She had to walk, whipped as she was by self-remorse. She went outside. She wouldn't go so far from the house that she wouldn't be able to run back inside and get the phone if it rang.

She walked down the steps and paced. All the places Joe could have gone kept flashing through her mind. She pictured it—Joe hot, sweaty, dusty, and possibly ill as he walked along a lonely road, while poor Michael, looking for him, drove along another road.

We were foolish, to say he could sleep overnight with his

cousins on the very day when he felt insecure in his new role as our son, she thought in self-chastisement. *We know the depth of commitment that an adoption entails, but he's a child, and he doesn't. By saying he could go, we reinforced his fear that we didn't need him. Then we had to start making love. Sure! Why not? It's what Michael and I do best no matter what's going on in our life. Other couples who have been together as long as we have would want a nap after picking berries on a hot August afternoon. But not the insatiable Danielses. If the world were coming to an end, we'd be making love as the planet expired. At the final explosion we'd be in ecstasy, thinking: Wow! What a terrific climax!*

She looked at a bit of rock that stuck up from the floor of needles underneath a pine tree and saw something sparkling next to it. Laura stared at the bit of metal gleaming in shadow, knowing the very second it caught her eye what it was.

A key. She went closer. Yes, a house key. She bent and lifted it. It was a key to the house in Beverly Hills. She had thrown it out the cabin door on New Year's Eve, to prove to Michael that she would never want to go back. The shifting weather of the months between then and now had pushed the key farther from the house than she could have thrown it and at some point tucked it under the rock for safekeeping. Should she tuck it away somewhere else, to keep as a memento? No, because in a very small way that would be like holding onto the Michael Daniels stores. Instead of a memento, the house key would be a symbol to her—a symbol of indecision.

She drew back her hand and looked ahead, to see how far she could toss the key this time. *When I throw this away, I'll try to throw away any desire I have to own the stores, to have a key back to the past.*

182

She was about to send the key flying when she changed her mind. She brought her hand down in front of her face and looked at what she held. A key! You needed a key to start the motor on the pontoon. Had Joe taken the boat and gone out on the lake?

She ran inside and went to where Michael kept the key to the pontoon's motor. It was gone. She thought hard: Joe knew how to operate the boat competently. There was no cause to worry on that score. Michael probably hadn't thought of this possibility, though, just as she hadn't until she found the old house key, which she now dropped into a wastebasket. Should she stay here and wait for Michael to call, as he surely would very soon? Then she would tell him where Joe might be and he would get someone with a boat to take him out on the lake.

That all made sense. But she thought also about how large Lake Pactola was. It was a lonely lake, even in the warm nights of summer. There was no development around it. It was vast and pristine, with numerous hidden coves at its shores, places where an unhappy child could anchor a boat and sit waiting—waiting for his mom and dad to come get him and convince him that they really were his mom and dad.

She would not wait. She would go to him herself. But how? She had driven Michael's truck only twice before, and both times she had felt uncomfortable doing it. The truck felt alien to her senses, hands, and feet. This was no time to try to come to terms with it. She could borrow a car, but even so she could drive only to one part of the lake —the point of the pontoon's departure.

Okay, I'll take one of the horses, she decided. She didn't even have to go back inside the house. Having been berry picking, she was dressed for riding, in jeans and socks and leather tennis shoes. She walked fast to where the horses were kept. She looked down as she went, concentrating on the task she was confronting. It wouldn't be easy. There wasn't foot access at many parts of the lake. The shoreline could be treacherous for a rider, with steep embankments and lots and lots of rocks.

Laura had never ridden a horse alone. This new experience, despite her worries, was special. She was by herself except for this splendid animal, which knew her and responded to her touch. She felt strong and independent, and as she rode, the future—her place in the future—was clarified for her. She leaned forward and patted the horse's neck. *We belong here, you and I,* she silently told her friend. Sitting back up, she looked around at the serenely beautiful place where she, Michael, Joe, and the baby belonged. There was a smile lighting her face because besides what she now realized about the future, she simply could not sit astride her horse without feeling that the world was good, life was an exhilarating adventure, and her problems would soon be resolved.

As if she were being rewarded for this faith, she was able to maneuver the horse down to the lake with relative ease. Then, rounding a curve of embankment, she saw the pontoon, anchored in a cove. Best of all, Michael was on the pontoon with Joe. He sprang from boat to shore when he saw her approach and reached her when she was still some distance from the boat. Joe had chosen a spot where the three of them had anchored the boat and picnicked frequently, and Laura could see that Michael had borrowed a motorboat to get to him.

Laura dismounted. She and Michael walked her horse toward the boat, with Laura holding the reins and Michael holding Laura's waist. Michael asked how she had known that Joe was here, and she said she'd looked for the pontoon's key and discovered that it wasn't in the house. Then she asked how he had decided to look for Joe at Pactola.

"Do you remember the Hansel and Gretel fairy tale?" Michael asked. "How the kids left a trail of bread crumbs when they went into the dark and evil woods? Joe did a Black Hills update on that story." Michael explained that Joe had actually dropped raspberries along the side of the road as he walked toward Pactola. Then he left the empty pail at the edge of the road, where it turned off and led down to the small boat slips.

They stopped walking. Joe had finally jumped onto the shore and was walking slowly toward them.

Laura hugged the boy and heard his quiet and sincere apology for having worried her. "I think that was very clever of you, honey, to drop a trail of berries so Dad would know you were at the lake." Turning to Michael, she said, "If we could market your eyesight and perception we'd be multimillionaires. I can't get over your seeing the berries and figuring out why they were there."

"I can't take that much credit." He grinned. "As soon as I got out to the main road, I suspected Joe had gone to the pontoon. I didn't know about the dropped berries until he told me. I did see the pail beside the road, which confirmed my suspicion, though. I also suspected you'd be too worried about Joe to bake a pie. Was I right?"

A pie. The preheated oven. Laura said, "Oh, my gosh! I left the oven on. I didn't bake the pie, but I thought I was going to and turned the oven on."

"I'll go turn it off!" Joe offered eagerly. "I'll ride the horse home, okay?"

Laura was skeptical, and her first instinct was to say no. It was a long ride, and Joe had not been out on a horse alone except when he rode very near their home. But he looked so eager to make up for what he had done, by doing

185

her this favor, that she hated to rob him of the opportunity.

"It's all right with me if it's all right with your dad," she said.

"Be careful. Keep to the side of the road, and ride slowly," Michael said.

"And don't look for a shortcut," Laura added, handing Joe the reins.

"As soon as you get home, call your aunt and tell her you're okay," Michael instructed Joe.

Then they were alone, walking with their arms around each other. "What a day!" Michael said musingly. "I feel as if I became a father."

"Overall, it's been a good day," Laura said. "Honey, we're so blessed. Michael, I want you to do something. Please sell the stores. We don't need to hold onto Michael Daniels as a crutch—something to run back to if times get rough. Really we don't. And I won't feel different after the baby is born."

They stopped walking and faced each other. "Laura, if you're being brave, for my sake . . ."

"I'm not! I'm not being brave at all. I love the place I call home, and I don't want to live anywhere else. Michael, I promise you that I'll never ask you to take me back. When I'm old and my bones ache from the cold, I might want long winter vacations in Southern California. But even then the Black Hills will be home to me. If I were alone—if you became smitten by a buxom little hussy with a butterfly tattooed on her fanny and ran off with her to . . . where would you run off to?"

"Mm, Mexico probably," Michael said thoughtfully.

"And you ran off with her to Mexico, and I *never* saw you again, I'd stay here. This would be my home. Now kiss me. The kiss will be your pledge to sell the stores."

186

Michael leaned down and kissed Laura gingerly, only touching her with innocently puckered lips. Then his strong arms came around her waist in a protective circle, and her hands met at the back of his neck.

"Laura," Michael said, "you did something for me today that was wonderful. I won't forget it as long as I live. Do you want to know what it was?"

Thinking that he would praise her for making a firm commitment about the future, she said happily, "Sure I do!"

"You mounted your horse and rode by yourself to where your son was—to where you were needed. When I saw you, I was overwhelmed. Laura, do you realize how far you've come? A year ago children, horses, wild raspberry fields, lakes and pontoons, hardworking people trying to decorate their homes on shoestring budgets—none of those were part of your world. You came into the Black Hills like a pilgrim, bent on adapting to the new land. And oh, honey, how you've adapted! Besides all that, you're absolutely gorgeous in the saddle."

She said nothing, simply nuzzling him, her nose and lips at the evening bristle beginning to shadow his warm jaw.

"Have you ever thought how lovely it would be to make love on a pontoon?" Michael asked. He hinted at what her answer should be by slipping his hands down over her hips and gently pulling her more snugly against him.

"Michael, Joe will be waiting for us."

"Mmm, he can wait a little while. Come on." He released her, only to take her hand and lead her toward the boat.

"I was thinking, earlier, that we're insatiable for an old married couple," Laura said musingly, looking up at Michael's beloved face. "I thought that if the world came to an end, we'd probably make love right up to the final second."

Michael moved her hand, which he was holding, to the back of his waist. When her fingers slipped into his pocket, he let go of her hand so he could put his arm around her shoulder and be closer to her. "I don't think the world's coming to an end, not in the next billion years anyhow. But I do think I smell roses. Do you?" he asked.

"I'll tell you when I'm on the boat." She laughed. She made the small leap to the pontoon, then took a long, heady sniff of the clean lake air. Oh, yes. Roses. Uncannily sweet-scented and beautiful roses. And in the predusk sky, stars. She opened her arms to Michael.

Candlelight
Ecstasy Romances™

$1.95 each

Fans of JAYNE CASTLE rejoice— this is her biggest and best romance yet!

From California's glittering gold coast, to the rustic islands of Puget Sound, Jayne Castle's longest, most ambitious novel to date sweeps readers into the corporate world of multimillion dollar real estate schemes—and the very *private* world of executive lovers. Mixing business with pleasure, they make passion *their* bottom line.

384 pages $3.95

Don't forget Candlelight Ecstasies, for Jayne Castle's *other* romances!